rocky point

Murders

an anthology of short stories involving
murder, mayhem and madness...

NOIR
PRESS

Rocky Point Murders is published by:
Noir Press
1850 Gough Street, #302
San Francisco, California 94109

Edited by Walter Randall Albers
Illustrations by Heidi McGurrin
Cover Art by Catherine Lise Miller

ISBN 0-9711727-0-6
Printed in the United States of America

DEDICATION

Dedicated to Maxine Shore
Who brought us together and gave us the courage to try

CONTENTS

FOREWORD

This small volume partially documents how, for nearly two centuries, Rocky Point has drawn twisted, vengeful, and homicidal souls to its unique beauty.

Rocky Point's sinister mystique was largely forgotten until the body of Professor Orsotti, a reclusive historian who lived in a cabin near Rocky Point, was found in 1936, several yards away from his head. His murder continues to baffle authorities.

The founder of our society was one of the first to enter Professor Orsotti's cabin following the discovery of his body. Among Orsotti's personal papers, Our Founder uncovered a hidden journal in which the professor had recorded the disturbing history of Rocky Point.

In his first entry, he notes sightings of small brown people in the shadows of Palo Colorado Canyon's redwoods. Their dress was that of the Rumsen tribe of Native Americans. Now extinct, the Rumsen occupied coastal lands from what is now Carmel to the Little Sur River. They were also known as the Carmeleños. Their rivals, the Esselen, controlled the area south from the Little Sur to Lucia.

Professor Orsotti's anthropological research shows that the gentle grassland just south of Rocky Point was the battleground of these warring tribes. Their war-making consisted of lines of warriors yelling and throwing stones at each other. Once the supply of stones was exhausted, the battle was over. Conflict between the Rumsen and the Esselen was gestural rather than lethal.

While the first entry is executed in vivid black, the second, written in the burnt orange of dried blood, records the arrival in the late eighteenth century of what the Professor calls "the mission imperialists." They regarded the lands south of the Carmel River with superstitious horror and gave it the name, "Sur."

Both the Rumsen and the Esselen peoples were coerced into the mission system. Orsotti's archeological investigations near Rocky Point produced abundant evidence that the grasslands where the Rumsen and the Esselen fought became killing fields for runaway mission Indians. A trail running behind what is now the Rocky Point Restaurant was blocked to seal them in, and "Horseback Imperial Trackers" were able to outrun any Indian on foot. They savaged the brown people — killing, beating, and returning the survivors to Padre Serra. The Professor reports some nights he could hear their ghostly screams in Palo Colorado Canyon.

The third entry, in original black ink, has the title, "Contrabandista" and describes the exploits of Captain Juan Bautista Rogers Cooper who arrived in California in 1823. At first, Cooper made his living killing otters until they were declared extinct in 1841. After the Gold Rush, he lost most of his holdings except the El Sur Ranch south of the Little Sur River.

Cooper became a smuggler. High customs duties made it profitable for him to off load cargo from China and the Sandwich Islands onto small boats and dock them inland on the Big Sur River. He built a trail up the coast, a portion of which passed through what is now the site of the restaurant at Rocky Point. Vaqueros on horseback carried the contraband to Monterey and returned with the proceeds, gold for Cooper at El Sur Ranch.

The lead Vaquero, Arturo "Pepe" Jaquez, skimmed some of the Captain's gold. At Rocky Point, Cooper confronted the embezzler. Jaquez was hanged from the tallest cypress at Rocky Point and never cut down. His body hung until it dropped in a pile below. Professor Orsotti's entry about Captain Cooper closes with, "The empty noose remained there as a reminder to anyone who thought of crossing the Captain."

One of the last entries in the journal describes the work of the Notley brothers, William and Godfrey. In the 1880's, they built a landing where lumber and tanbark, harvested in Palo Colorado Canyon, were loaded onto ships south of Rocky Point. Notley's Landing was home to Ma Swetnam's boarding house where seaman and others got bed and board.

Ma must have been a real sight. "My research indicates," Orsotti writes, "that Ma was so large that she couldn't feed herself with a spoon. She threw her food at her mouth from a distance of two feet. According to observers, Ma never missed."

The bar and dance hall at Notley's Landing sucked in the lumber and limekiln workers' pay. Drink loosened lethal prejudices against the recent influx of Italian workers. "At Sunday sunrise," the Professor records, "the Rocky Point woods were littered with the bodies of the victims of drunken violence, mostly Italian. Killings were most often accomplished by knifing. Victims were also lynched in the same cypress grove where Pepe Jaquez was hanged. Some men were beaten to death by bare fists."

Professor Orsotti's last Journal entry in March 1936 is the lengthiest. It opens with a brief history of the building of Highway One from the Carmel River to San Luis Obispo (with convict labor). Road gangs widened the cut north of the Palo Colorado and Orsotti objected, since the road bosses were not respecting significant archeological sites. He protested to local authorities and was ignored.

Apparently, the professor took matters into his own hands. The last two pages of the journal say:

When the crews were allowed to rest, I was free to walk among them, asking if they had found anything of archeological interest. I became friendly with Billy Boleen, a convict sentenced to life for murder. Billy told me, in his barely literate way, that the conditions under which the men were forced to work were inhuman. When his comrades complained, they were beaten in the bunkhouses at night.

His bunkmate, Chance Dalton, wrote a letter to Eleanor Roosevelt detailing the atrocities. Apparently his letter didn't get by the censor. Chance Dalton was found dead several hundred yards from the bunkhouse one morning. The "bulls," as Billy called the guards, said Chance Dalton tried to escape. Chance made a second copy of his letter 'just in case' and gave it to Billy, if he would promise to get it out. He will pass it to me tomorrow.

Our plan is for me to appear with a newspaper. Billy will insert Chance's letter into the pages when the guards are not watching. I have promised to get it to Mrs. Roosevelt.

The professor's body was found two days later. According to our independent research, the day before the professor's death, seven guards shot Billy Boleen as he ran toward Rocky Point. The District Attorney ruled the shooting of the unarmed convict as "justifiable homicide."

The mission of our society is to continue the work of Professor Orsotti. We are mindful of the personal risks that that entails. For this reason, membership in our society carries the privilege of total anonymity.

Knowing the risks that attend our efforts and the evil mystique of Rocky Point, our collaboration with the Carmel

Writers' Workshop had one condition: the names of the real actors in the stories that follow have been changed. This will protect the writers.

Cold, Hard Cash

BY ROGER HENWEDGE

Cold, Hard Cash
BY ROGER HENWEDGE

Headlights swept over Tony's head as he scrunched down in the front seat. The parking lot was now empty except for his Camaro and Rocky Point Restaurant's pick-up truck.

All clear. The money'll be in my hands in just a few minutes. He bounded out of the car, opened the trunk. A light revealed a tire, tool kit, golf bag with clubs and a tightly-tied black plastic bag. That was Marlene. Not the Marlene that he'd enjoyed wild sex with a couple hours before. This was a doubled-over, broken-spined Marlene he created after strangling her.

She'd always been convenient and comfortable for him. She still was, as a neat compact bag he shouldered across the parking lot. This is as it had to be. Like fate, he thought. I've worked too hard, waited too long for it not to go this way.

As Tony rounded the back of the building, the rumble and whine of the refrigerator compressors drowned out the roar of the waves hitting the rocky coast below. This night was just like the others he'd bartended at this Big Sur landmark. Tens of thousands, he figured, decades of smiling at customers, listening to their crap. Only now, this night, was the pay-off.

Tony threw the sack on top of one of the large trash bins, unlocked the kitchen door. Better take her in, just in case. In total darkness he started through the prep kitchen. He knew the way by heart.

His foot hit something metal which clattered across the cement floor. Damn, when will those beaners learn to hang up pans, put things where they belong?

He moved more slowly now, turning into the storage area. A loud thud. Another. Tony froze. When a few seconds later he heard scraping and scratching, he decided that raccoons were foraging for food in one of the trash bins.

His heart pounded faster as his hand found the walk-in freezer door handle. His whole future was inside. Opening the heavy door triggered a light which illuminated a six-by-eight sheet-metalled room filled with everything from tortillas to fruit, from bacon and sausage to ice cream. He didn't even feel the cold blast from the compressor fans that hit him as he parted the heavy plastic curtain. The excitement of getting this close to five hundred grand erased the forty degree temperature drop.

He stepped in, dumped Marlene on the floor. "Where's the money?" Tony muttered to himself. He pushed aside bags of coffee beans, found half a dozen white boxes, looked in each: cheesecake, they were all cheesecake. His elbow caught the corner of a large plastic sack of French fries which tipped over and spread like chopsticks across the floor. "The damned shrimp! That's what she said. The money's with the shrimp!"

His head almost hit the bare bulb as he pivoted to another row of shelves along the back. A blast of frigid air hit his head, tangling his thick black hair. He squatted, pushed aside cans of crab meat, boxes of garlic salt, saw a large box stamped Mexico, pulled it out and ripped open the top. "Prawns, I'm getting close." He pushed it aside and pulled out and opened another box. Only this time he saw green – a layer of green one-hundred dollar bills. Spread out flat and beautiful, like a Warhol pop-art painting.

He stopped breathing, as if he'd been hit in the stomach. "This is it! Five-hundred thousand! Cold, hard cash! Set for life!"

The heavy plastic curtain hit his side as the door slammed shut and the light went out. Tony didn't move, still stunned, hypnotized. In his mind's eye he saw the layer of green hundred dollar bills. He had five-hundred thousand dollars, all his, no strings. But I'd better get out of here. Get rid of Marlene and head to Mexico.

He pushed the door's inside opener. It didn't move. Pushed the knob again, this time leaning hard against it. Still no movement.

Nobody's here to close the door, so it must be stuck. Maybe with light I can see what's wrong. He felt for the inside switch, pushed it. The five-hundred grand was still there, still beautiful. He reached down to finger one of the hundreds, couldn't, it was frozen into a block with he didn't know how many others. Never mind that now. Got to get out of here.

He pushed the knob every which way, finally stepping back and throwing his whole weight against the door. No movement.

The door had never stuck before. He'd been in this freezer thousands of times. For the extra ice on weekends. And when he'd taken inventory for the kitchen manager, Hector Fernandez, he'd kept the door closed and opened it easily with the inside knob.

"It's a safety knob, dammit, it's got to work!" he shouted, as he pushed in vain. "Unless...." The word hung in the frigid air. Unless there was someone else in the restaurant who had shut and locked the door. He knew a piece of metal or even a large stick pushed through the outside handle would keep the latch from operating.

He sat on the cold metal floor as he accepted what seemed the only explanation. There was someone, and that someone wanted to kill him. He got up and began beating on the door.

"Open this door, you bastard, open this door! I'll cut you in – give you twenty-five thou right off the top – now open this door!" He shouted till he was hoarse. Screamed, pounded, paused and listened, but heard only the roar of the compressors and the whirring of the fans.

He stopped. Exhausted. This wasn't working. Got to think. Damn, I'm freezing. Got to conserve body heat. He had a hard time buttoning his shirt tight around his neck and zippering up his jacket because his fingers were stiff. He made fists, flexed them open and closed. Got to keep moving. His hand across his forehead knocked off beads of sweat that had turned to ice.

He sat on an ice cream container. Who the hell's out there? I know there's someone right outside this door. But who'd want to kill me? If I can figure that out, I'll know what to say. Who knows beside Marlene? He glanced at the black plastic bag. Could she have told someone? Could someone have overheard us this afternoon?

It had been a slow day. The lunch rush was over and he'd sent Marlene to the liquor storage room to restock the Merlot. Her face was flushed as she set some bottles on the bar.

"Come out on the patio, will ya?"

Two customers were nursing their drinks in the gazebo, but otherwise they were alone.

"Tony, this is big. When I was getting the wine, I heard your friend Lou and some other guy talking in the men's room – you know that wall's like paper, well, they're paying someone in the kitchen to keep a box in the walk-in freezer overnight." Her lips were quivering.

"So?" He took a drag on a cigarette.

"Five-hundred thousand. The box has five-hundred thousand – cash they said, and the feds who followed them into Big Sur are in the restaurant now, and they're afraid to try to get it out. Plan on picking it up tomorrow morning."

"You sure?" Tony's mouth gaped open. "Cash?"

"Yes, definitely, that's what they said." Her eyes darted back toward the bar. She sidled closer. "You have a key, I don't, so we could come back tonight. We'd split the money, or...," she paused as she touched his arm, "we could go to Mexico and never worry the rest of our lives. If you got bored, you could open your own bar, and I could waitress, so we'd have our own place for a change, run it just the way we'd want to."

That dream about Mexico was hers, not Tony's. Women are like that, he thought. If you don't throw a fit when they say something, they think you agree. When he heard her lay it all out, he knew he had to take care of her. He wasn't going to spend the rest of his life with that broad, and he sure as hell wasn't going to split the five-hundred thousand. But he didn't blink.

"Great! Let's celebrate. After work come over to my place, we'll toss down a few, get it on, and make plans. If you're right, we're set...for life!"

She squeezed his arm and we went back in to finish the shift. Could someone have heard them? Maybe down below at the firepit? She wouldn't tell anybody, so someone must've heard.

He wiped his nose, but couldn't feel it. Gotta get up and move. Got to keep movin' so I don't freeze.

Tony stood, stomped his feet, then braced himself against the door and ran in place. Turned around and walked in a tight circle, slipping on the frozen fries. Getting dizzy, the motor's roar seemed to lessen. Then he started shivering, his whole body shook, and he could hear his heart beating. But it wasn't right. Wasn't regular. Keep focused, he told himself. Ignore the pain.

And then there was Louie, standing right there, a small imp of a man, round, red face, hair parted in the middle, looking nothing like the scam artist he was.

"Hey, how ya doin'? Close any big deals lately? I got a hell of a trick for ya, cost ya' ten grand though. But it's a sure thing, fast turn-around on some strawberries over in Salinas that won't make it past the weekend. I need a buyer now."

He got up close to Tony's face. "Hey, ya ain't lookin' too good here. Sharp guy like you got to keep up appearances."

"Louie, is it you? Did you slam the door? Are you tryin' to kill me?"

Louie laughed. "Me? Just because you screwed me over on that Dodge van deal? Kill ya over somethin' like that? Give me a break!"

And he vanished. What's going on? Louie was never here. Somebody's playing with my head. Keep walking, don't sleep, walk faster. Feeling weak, better eat something.

He hit a muffin pack against the shelf. The muffins scattered onto the floor. Hard as rocks. Sucked on the edge of one but it never softened. Maybe one of those breakfast sausages'll work. Put it in his mouth. Slowly he tasted something, something spicy. Rolled his tongue around it over and over and finally when he bit down a small end broke off and he swallowed. He did that a couple times. His eyes kept closing. Getting sleepy. Can't do that, can't do that, that's the end if I do that. Keep walking. He pushed his legs to keep moving, but it was nothing like walking, couldn't feel anything. Getting dizzier. And then there was Ma.

"Mary, mother of God, what have you gotten yourself into now? What is it?" She paused. "I'm waiting." A pretty-faced, pasta-filled woman of fifty, arms folded across her ample bosom, stood stolidly at his side. "I'm waiting, Antonio."

His blue lips quivered. "I don't know, Ma. Tried to do what you and dad taught."

"You sure did. Your no-good father ran the numbers, and you set up a half-assed operation here in the bar at Rocky Point. I see similarities. But you got a little too big for your britches is what I think. Playing around with those high-rollers from Pebble; they were never our crowd. Your father knew every one of his customers, salt of the earth people they were. None of those dot-comers you've glad-handed the last few years. They made it fast, will lose it just as fast, and I bet you're caught right in the middle, is that it? I'm waiting!"

"No, ma, I swear, I played all of 'em fair and square. Skimmed a little off the top from the other barkeeps, but I was entitled, bein' head bartender and all."

"No matter." Her face hardened. "No matter what you and your father did, neither of you piss-ants made enough money to fill a barrel and go over Niagara. Never saw such lameness in my life. You haven't been to confession in a while, have ya? Mary, mother of God, what's to become of ya?"

Tony blinked. Ma was gone. Breathing was hard. His lungs burned with cold. When he exhaled, he choked and coughed. Room spun round and round. Light dimmed. Got to get out of here! Got to stop the cold! He grabbed pieces of shrimp, pushed them into the fans. If I can stop the blowers....The metal diced and spit the shrimp back as fast as he pushed them in.

Sat down. Couldn't keep eyes open. "Can't sleep! Can't sleep!" he yelled, and the room was turning and there was Marlene.

"Well, you've got it all now. The cold, hard cash, it's all yours. Don't have to share it with me. Five-hundred thousand. Sitting there beside you. 'Pretty as a picture,' I heard you say. You said we'd be set for life. Didn't quite work out that way for either of us, did it? You'll be joining me shortly. Have a bad trip."

Tony tried to reach for Marlene, hit the door, leaned against it, his body a solid block of pain. Eyes closed, his tongue stuck to the roof of his mouth. As he fell asleep he heard the music of mariachis.

Six the next morning, Hector Fernandez, the kitchen manager, opens the freezer, folds the frozen Tony into a black trash sack, takes him out and dumps him into the large garbage bin. He does the same with the other bag. The bin's contents would be picked up and buried at the county landfill a few hours later.

Driving south on Highway 101, he pats the still frozen box on the seat beside him.

Stupid gringos! Think if they bribe you with two hundred dollars you'll be dumb enough not to open a box. I'll be in Tijuana in nine hours, home in another two. I'll wake Maria and the kids and tell them the news. We can open our restaurant, Punta Rocosa del Sur. It will be a great success, a new Rocky Point! I'll keep using the classic cheese butter recipe for the cheese bread; that was Marlene's favorite.

Perfect
BY GRETA G. KOPP

Perfect

BY GRETA G. KOPP

A sleek hull, streamlined, smooth. Wallace Avery's boat. Perfection her name, her attitude. Wally liked his women the same way.

He stood on the flying bridge of the sixty-two-foot cabin cruiser, shoulders squared, eyes watchful, hands planted firmly at the helm, ready to correct any deviation from course. A change in the weather? He'd be ready. He controlled his women like that, too.

Calm water today, all around the Monterey Peninsula, not much wind, temperature in the sixties, humidity low. A typical August day.

Twin diesels hummed as they carried Perfection through a blue glass sea. The sky, dressed scantily in ruffled white, stretched endlessly to the western horizon where a thick fogbank waited to make its nightly move inland. By dinner time the entire coast would be socked in. Wallace and Gayle had spent most of the day on the water, sailing as far south as the Point Sur lighthouse and were now headed north, back towards Monterey Bay, Perfection's home port.

"Great day to be out," he said. He glanced at his wife, Gayle, who stood a few feet away pumping ten-pound dumbbells. "Why did you bring those damn things on board, again?"

She smiled, and kept pumping. "One and two and three and four. I always do, Wally. You know the old saying, 'never put off till tomorrow....'"

"Yeah, yeah," he grunted. "Perhaps if you'd started ten years ago it might have done some good."

She ignored his sarcasm, sat down and laid the weights beside her.

"That's enough for now." She took several deep breaths. "I feel better already."

"Okay, so why the sudden desire to see Rocky Point today? Lucky for you we've got a calm sea or I'd stay farther out. Dangerous as hell around there. Too many shipwrecks to suit me."

"Let's call it a celebration. A beginning, an end, and another beginning."

"Riddles don't amuse me. Get to the point."

"I wanted to talk, Wally. I never get you alone long enough to have a decent conversation."

"I'm a busy man these days."

"You're always a busy man. I thought getting you out here, out in the boat - I know how much you love it - without any distractions," without other women, "would give us a chance to...to...well, discuss things."

"Things?"

Gayle knew he had already lost interest. A familiar pattern that started...how many years ago? She couldn't remember, but the pain was familiar, and recurring. He studied the gentle swell of the ocean, from port to starboard, and back again. "No wind," he commented, more to himself than to Gayle. "Not too many days like this out here, I can tell you. Let's hope it lasts or that blasted fog out there will roll in before we get back."

She knew he didn't expect an answer. She knew little about yachting, but everything about him. Twenty-five years makes a good student. She watched the movement of his head as he scanned the horizon, the sky, the endless stretch of blue water. He stared ahead where off in the distance, slightly to starboard, the crags and boulders of Rocky Point loomed into view. Dangerously close now.

Back to port, his eyes lingered on a lone fisherman close to the horizon. Occasionally, the boat disappeared into the fogbank, only to reappear minutes later. A seagull squealed overhead then dipped to the water. Wallace followed its path. They have much in common, Gayle decided, the seabird searching for that familiar fluorescent flash and the man to whom she had been married for what seemed an eternity. But Wally's hunger was of a different nature.

"She'll be in port before us," Wally said, pointing to the fisherman.

"Okay with me. View's to be enjoyed on a day like this." She peered at the approaching fogbank. "But not for long."

He glanced briefly at his wife then asked, "What did you want to talk about?" He didn't wait for a reply. "You were right, you know, I needed to relax, get out of the office. Was that it? I'm tired of conferences, tired of talking to incompetent idiots without a goddamn brain in their heads."

So don't bother me with your problems. Gayle read the unspoken message in his tone of voice. She had deciphered his warnings for years, as soon as the honeymoon wore off, perhaps three months into their marriage. Time for her to join the ranks of the discarded. But she was a patient woman.

She watched his hands on the wheel, aware of his physical strength. A tall, slender man, he kept himself in excellent shape. Tennis, workouts at the gym; his body belonged to a much younger man. Only the sketchy lines at the sides of his mouth and around his eyes told the truth. Sun, he would say when she had touched them. And then he'd laugh. But the sun could not be blamed for the glint of steel she saw in his pale eyes when he pushed her hand away.

Years ago, those blue eyes had driven her wild, his bronzed skin and taut belly turned her to putty. She had believed him perfect in every way, this prime specimen, her husband. It was she who suggested the boat's name. "Perfection," so in keeping with its captain. Now she despised every muscular inch of him. She hated the sham their marriage had become, shunned everything they had once shared, including this miserable vessel. But Wallace would never admit there was anything wrong between them. That would suggest failure. He had no failures. Splitting up was never an option. His hands played the wheel. Just a light, controlled touch. He caressed the smooth finish of varnished teak, let the perfect curve take a momentary slide through his fingers before bringing it back on course. His course. His lips hinted at a smile. Control was his passion in life.

It's her, her body he feels, she thought. The latest gem in his collection. He's caressing her, guiding her, stroking, feeling her response to his hands. She could imagine his erection beneath the immaculate white pants, sense the blurring of his vision behind the dark glasses, picture the images running through his mind.

Bile rose up in her throat but she choked it back. This was a time to stay calm. Her clenched fingers itched to wipe the smile off his lips. She flexed and unflexed them before they became a fist and lunged against his mouth.

Standing abruptly, she leaned against the rail and stared into the water. Distorted shadows darted back and forth beneath the surface, probably fish. But, to her, they seemed a reflection of herself, a woman for too many years uncertain which direction to take in her life. But that was about to change.

Perfection's bow parted the ocean with barely a whisper. Only the hum of the engines and the occasional cry of gulls stirred the silence. Still too much noise for what she had to say. And this time she wanted his full attention.

She stepped forward, reached behind the wheel, grabbed the ignition key and turned it off.

"What the hell...?" Wally glared at her, his mouth stretched to a snarl.

"I'm divorcing you!" Gayle announced, her voice pitched to a quiet scream. Without another word, she threw herself back onto the seat before she lost control. Her fingers trembled as she tried to stem the rush of blood to her cheeks, her knees felt weak, she wanted to throw up. There, she'd done it, said it. Those dreaded words. She took a deep breath. Not too difficult after all, really. And now it was over. Done, finished. But, of course, it wasn't over. It would never be over.

He turned and scowled at her, his hands gripping the wheel, the skin taut.

"What the hell? In the middle of the goddamn ocean? For Chrissakes, Gayle, couldn't you have found a better time for this?" He turned the ignition back on, but kept his speed down. "Do you want us to drift into those rocks, run aground? In case you haven't noticed, you stupid woman, we're too close to Rocky Point to be fucking around with the engines."

"I don't care where we are," she snapped back with uncharacteristic courage. "I've made up my mind. And don't try to shut me out, pretend you don't hear me."

"Since when did you get the right to make up your mind about anything that concerns me?" He paused, chewing his lower lip. "Did you think long and hard about where you might choose to have another of your menopausal, bitchy arguments? No, of course you didn't. That would take brains, and that seagull out there has you beat hands down in that department. What the hell's the matter with you?"

"I've had enough. I want my half of everything. In cash. No matter what it takes."

He gave her a quick glance and laughed. "Go to hell!"

"I've talked to a lawyer."

"I don't care if you've had a conference with God. No divorce!"

He adjusted his cap, then increased speed. "We're going back in."

Gayle took a deep breath. "I won't change my mind. Intimidation won't work. I'm fed up with you, with your...your bimbos." She thrust out her chin. "I've got proof...photos, tapes of your cozy little rendezvous at the hotels around town. My lawyer can fry you."

Wallace laughed. "Son of a bitch," he said, "I didn't think you had it in you. You've had me tailed?"

He idled the engines, allowing Perfection to wallow in the gentle swell, then moved to stand towering over her. He bent down and peered into her face. "You don't stand a chance in hell. You try to divorce me and it's you who'll get fried. Hear me? You'll end up without a stinking penny. Just try me."

She recognized his bluff but fear rippled through her.

"You don't scare me, Wally."

"Wanna bet?" He bent down and slapped her hard across the face, again, and then again.

"Stop it, Wally. Stop! Please stop," she pleaded. She raised her hands to ward off the next blow. He backed off and she pressed her trembling fingers against her face, felt the heat and pain rising through her flesh.

"Turn around and look up at the top of those rocks," he commanded. "That's where I made the most stupid mistake of my life. We got engaged at the Rocky Point restaurant. That's why you wanted to come out here, isn't it? To remind me of my commitment. Make me look like a fool."

Who's really the fool? Gayle wondered. What other woman would put up with the Wallys of this world for so damned long? None of her friends. They had told her as much. But she had loved him so completely, had never given up hope that she could save their marriage.

"You gave me this beautiful ring, there," Gayle said, holding out her left hand.

He grabbed it and bent back her third finger until she thought it might break. "Set me back fifteen thousand bucks. Twenty-five years ago. I don't forget things like that."

She glanced down at her engagement ring, watched the sun's rays splash fire across the facets of the flawless, three-carat diamond. It had become a symbol of his power over her.

He grabbed her chin and pushed his face up against hers. "Surprised you with that perfect little bauble, didn't I, baby? God knows, you were worth it back then." He moved his eyes down her body. "Now look at you. Flab, wrinkles. But you're still my wife and you don't walk away from me until I say you can. Got that?" He hit her again and she felt the blood spurt out of her nose. He laughed, moved back to the helm, increased speed to eight knots.

In spite of her resolve, tears trickled down her face. She tasted the salt and blood on her lips. She stared up at him and saw what he had become. She would have forgiven him his first affair; one mistake should not be allowed to ruin a marriage. But others followed, one after another, each woman progressively younger. In trying to recover his youth, he shed his conscience, along with any sense of decency he might once have possessed. Respect for his wife, had there ever been any, withered away.

Weeks had passed since Gayle made her decision to divorce him, but terror held back her pronouncement. What would he say? Do to her? How could she approach him? Then she hit on the idea of coming out here on the boat. The sea had a calming influence on Wallace. He relaxed, became almost decent. They seemed to communicate better when his hands guided Perfection out to sea. Gayle knew her husband wanted his freedom from her so he could continue playing the field. Perhaps, just perhaps, she had thought, he might see reason, agree to a divorce. Wrong again.

But keep going, she told herself, don't fade now. The worst is over. You've told him. She took another deep breath, then plunged ahead.

"I've known about them from the start," she said. Her hands gripped the rail at her sides. "Every one of them. How could you, Wally? You even brought them into our home, flaunted them in front of me."

"I wanted to remind you what kind of woman turns me on. Even thinking about making love to you is a bad dream. They're young, exciting. Take a good, long look at yourself, Gayle." He snickered. "Make the comparison, baby."

"It was always about you feeling good, wasn't it? It didn't matter how I felt. It was never about my needs, always yours. Well, I don't care what you need. Not anymore. I'm leaving you, and you're going to pay. Dearly! It's over."

"Don't kid yourself, my pet," he said, his eyes on the horizon. You get nothing. Hear me? Nothing. I earned every penny. I'll keep every penny."

Her voice grew faint. "You can't stop me."

"Watch me."

She took a deep breath and plunged ahead. "There's someone else in my life. I've already filed."

His fist hit the helm. "Shit! I'll kill you for this."

With amazing speed, Gayle ran from the seat to the steps and crashed down them, two at a time, onto the main deck. Seconds, that's all she had before he came after her. Enough time to follow through? She knew he needed to guide Perfection away from the rocks, re-set his course. Then he'd make his move.

She lunged toward the instrument panel, reached for the radio switch. Her hands trembled, but she managed to switch it on. Gasping, and trying to keep her voice low, she called out "Mayday! Mayday! Rocky Point," then switched the radio off.

She heard the engines slow way down. She turned and saw Wally's feet appear at the top of the steps. Had he heard her call for help? Quickly, she took the remaining steps down into the salon and moved behind the galley table, out of his reach.

He moved down after her, rushed into the salon like an angry bear and tried to grab her by the arm. But in the confined space his size worked against him. He became almost clumsy, making it easier for her to escape around the table and back up the steps to open space. He followed, moving faster now. She rushed for the steps and scurried back up to the flying bridge, her lungs gasping for air, her heart pounding.

He was on her heels. She felt his hands on her back shoving her forward. She crashed onto the bench seat. As she began to turn around, his fist connected with her chin, knocking her backwards, but it was a glancing blow, causing little damage to her already battered face.

"You bitch." He grabbed her arms. She pulled free and moved further back into the seat, her back arched over the railing, her hands clinging to the wet stainless steel.

She screamed, tried to escape, but he grabbed her arms, holding her tight, his fury palpable through the pressure of his fingers.

"You're hurting me."

"How dare you go behind my back." He was breathing hard now, his face livid.

"You're a bastard."

"You knew all along how I feel about divorce, how it screws up everything I've ever worked for."

"You used me, Wally."

"You just want my money."

"It's mine too."

"The hell it is. You won't get it. You'll die first."

He released his grip long enough for Gayle to scramble to her feet. She yanked her ring off her finger and shoved it under his nose. "Here's your ring, and here's what I think about it." She turned around and dropped it over the side into the water.

"What the shit?" Wally shoved her aside and leaned over the railing.

Gayle picked up one of the dumbbells from the seat and crashed it against the back of his skull. Wally slumped over the rail. She dropped the dumbbell over the side then lifted and pushed Wally's body until it fell free from the railing. He disappeared beneath the ocean, re-surfaced facedown, then drifted away from Perfection towards the horizon. Gayle watched him for only seconds, then dropped the second dumbbell over the side.

"The doctor said I could have a few minutes, Mrs. Avery. I'm Inspector Ramirez, Monterey County Sheriff's Department."

Gayle pulled herself up from the semi-conscious state between sleep and daydreaming. Not an unpleasant place to be, she thought, as she righted her head on the hospital pillow.

He stared at her battered face, and frowned. "How are you feeling?" he asked, moving toward the bed. He grabbed a chair from beside the wall and brought it with him. "Do you mind?"

She shook her head. "No."

"Looks like you took quite a beating."

She gave a half smile and touched her cheek. "It's okay," she said.

"I've been talking to the Coast Guard," he said. "They brought me up to date, about your distress call, their arrival on the scene shortly after. And I got an interesting report from a customer at Rocky Point restaurant. Some woman with binoculars, apparently whale watching. Said she saw you and your husband struggling on the boat."

Gayle raised her head from the bed, her eyes moist with tears, her mouth tight with anxiety. "My husband! Did they find him? Where is he? Poor Wally." She began to whimper, put her hand across her mouth, then collapsed back onto the pillows. "Oh my God, he's gone, isn't he?"

The sergeant laid a hand on her arm. "I'm very sorry, Mrs. Avery. The Coast Guard found no trace of him."

She looked up, her eyes suddenly fearful. "I think he was trying to kill me. He kept hitting me, over and over again." She fingered the bruises on her face.

"I think we'd better leave this until tomorrow," the sergeant said, standing. "You're still in shock. The doctor thinks you'll be able to go home by then. I'll want a complete account of everything that happened. If you can remember."

"How could I ever forget?"

"Then I'll see you some time tomorrow afternoon." He started to leave, stopped, turned around. "I almost forgot. You have another visitor. Your attorney's waiting outside."

"Do I have to see him now?" she complained. "I'm terribly tired. He'll want me to sign all kinds of papers and stuff. I don't think I can bear it."

"Then I'll tell him to come back later."

"No, no, never mind," she said, quickly. "I'll see him. But lawyers always talk too much. It's so fatiguing."

The sergeant smiled and left the room. Moments later, a tall, well-dressed man with a shock of thick, gray hair walked in. He closed the door and moved silently to the bed. He bent over and laid his lips on Gayle's forehead.

"How are you, my darling?" he asked.

"I survived," she said.

He touched the bruises on her face, then sat on the chair beside the bed. She moved her ringless left hand towards him. He lifted it up, patted it like a father soothing a distressed child.

"A dreadful loss," she said.

He brought her fingers to his lips. "Yes, but worth it." He leaned closer. "Because now we get it all."

She eased her hand away from his fingers and looked into his eyes. "We? What do you mean 'we'?"

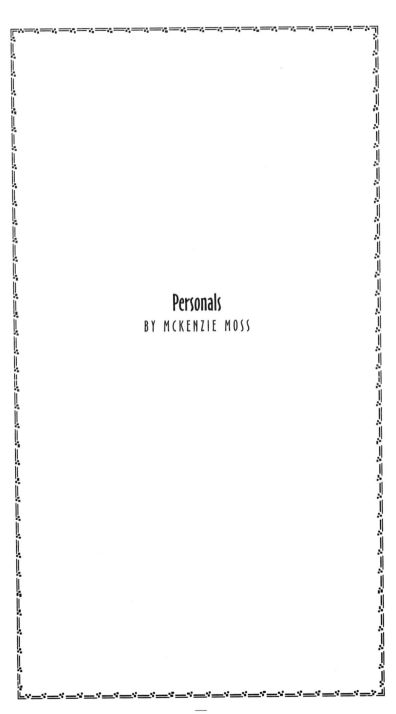

Personals

BY MCKENZIE MOSS

Personals
BY MCKENZIE MOSS

Buck Keller leaned against the edge of the window and watched frame apartment houses parade down Pacific Grove's hills; they marched in time to a foghorn's grunting dirge, their shapeless hulks sliding into the gray sea mist. Buck was one with the fog and buildings, without form, without edges. He couldn't shake a dark premonition, an omen as chill as the fog, stinking of salt and ripe fish, making his insides roll. He shivered as the scenes replayed themselves.

Eight months? A year? Before that, and before that. Buck felt his soul atomize into colorless particles of nothingness and mix with the dripping sky. He knew a next time would come, the succubi to emerge from Cimmerian recesses, to intone their singsong requiem, the rage to be unleashed, rage obliterating all reason, triggering the inevitable denouement.

The first time had been a chance meeting in a San Mateo bar. Two days later they lay in her bed; he recited a litany of despair and abandonment, festering sores he wouldn't let heal. She had sneered and told him to grow up for Christ-sake. She kept it up, her gibes tearing at him like the claws of a subterranean beast. Don't talk that way, he said. He heard the mantra ooze from the crevices of his mind, a dissonant chorus that swirled over him, strangling him. Buck had no choice — he had to stop her, stop them.

He recalled stumbling into the weeping night, racing to San Francisco in his VW. Police investigators, according to the newspaper, said the victim knew her killer, concluding that the couple's intimacy had been consensual. Hell yes, they always knew him, it was always consensual.

Lynn Ward sat at her dressing table wearing thick horn-rims and a wrap-around towel. The piano wire tension across her shoulders had almost vanished, thanks to a steaming bath and second glass of Chardonnay. It was delicious to be home, to be in her tiny Carmel cottage once more. She wished she'd never have to leave, that today's flight had been her last.

Chicago to San Francisco had been punctuated by delays, turbulence, and men-in-heat, assholes trapped in perpetual adolescence hitting on her and the other flight attendants. Even the short commuter hop to Monterey had been late, the whole day a lead weight that dragged her down. Lynn reached to dig her fingers into the orange fur of a cat sitting at her feet.

"I think momma deserves a night out, Panache."

The cat leaped into her lap and thrust his forepaws into the towel across her lower belly. An unexpected rush of carnal pleasure infused her.

"Whoa there, little man," her voice turned hoarse. She gentled the cat off her lap. He climbed onto the dresser to sit, his eyes darting between Lynn and the woman in the mirror. Lynn removed her glasses, retrieved a flaxen wig from a drawer, and fit it over her black pageboy. She worked the short blonde hair until it fell loose around her temples and neck. From a small case she took contact lenses, put drops into each and placed them into her washed-blue eyes.

Lynn inspected the mirror. A seductive, hazel-eyed blonde returned her stare and laughed a guttural, erotic laugh. Panache reacted as if a high voltage wire had struck him. Hair straight up, ears flat, he released a primeval yowl and arched his back.

"Crazy cat," Lynn grinned and reached for him. Panache hissed and smacked at her with his paw. A flash of pain, instant scarlet streaks on her palm.

"You son of a bitch!" She swung her hand, knocking him to the floor. Panache slunk away to cower under the bed while Lynn glowered at him and licked the salt-sweet scratches.

ROCKY POINT RESTAURANT
Sunday night. You: thirties, salt/pepper hair, brown eyes, Telluride T-shirt,flight jacket. Me: Meg Ryan, independent — don't tread on me. See you next Monday at Monterey Airport. UAL 10:25 to SF.

Buck perused the area around Gate 7 in Monterey's terminal building. Several passengers continued to stand in line at the nearby United ticket counter. He couldn't believe he was doing this, suckering for a personals ad, some wannabe movie star look-a-like. It had been her declaration of independence that hooked him: "...don't tread on me." He'd tread on her, more than she ever dreamed.

The clock read 10:05. Don't be so damned anxious. Buck flipped up the collar of his scuffed leather jacket, feeling as conspicuous as a teen-ager in church. He found an empty seat and plopped down, glancing at the dark-eyed woman beside him, then doing a double take when he realized she was breast-feeding an infant, all the while scolding in Spanish a fidgety toddler at her feet. Buck's groin tightened as he viewed the massive brown nipple under the demanding mouth. He wondered if he had been breast-fed, if that might have changed his life. Again he hated his mother, whoever and wherever she was.

Buck grabbed a stray section of the Monterey Herald from the floor. He pretended to read while he inventoried the passengers and stole glimpses of his neighbor's bosom. The mother detached her suckling baby and fixed her sooty eyes on Buck, giving him a suggestive smile while she pushed her blue-veined roundness into the brassiere.

Jesus, she's asking for it. He dragged his eyes away and searched the lobby. Give or take twenty women, every make and model, most alone. Action, lots of it. Maybe he should take this flight. The fantasy vanished as quick as it appeared, replaced by a sudden, oppressive sense of danger. He shuddered and shook it off, continuing his surveillance.

A thirty-something fox went through security and glanced at him, then away. It could be Meg, until he saw red hair peeking from under her fitted wool hat. He noticed other women talking into cellulars, fingering laptops. God, is this where we're headed? Stepford wives coupling with cell phones and PCs?

He felt like a stalker; sweat soaked his forehead, chest, under arms. Then again, he thought, I am a stalker. He got up and walked to the window dividing the passenger area from the rest of the terminal. He could see the twin engine Brasilia, passengers queued up to climb the stairway to the cabin, one of them a flight attendant he'd seen in the lobby coffee shop earlier, probably deadheading to work a flight out of San Francisco. She had thrown him a quick glance and a plastic smile. Almost pretty, with black pageboy hair, pale blue eyes magnified by coke bottle glasses. No Meg Ryan.

Another ten minutes and the plane's door closed, a tractor pulled the stairway free and the propellers spun. Buck stuffed his hands in his pockets and headed to the parking lot. So much for personals. Suckered.

Go to hell, Meg Ryan.

UAL
You were sexy Monday morning — flight jacket,
Levi's, blue button down, burning eyes. We're meant
to be. - *Meg*

Panache stood guard on the bedroom windowsill. Rain spit out of the black night, rattling against the panes. At the bathroom mirror, Lynn considered with satisfaction the nude, five-foot-six blonde with green eyes. Not any longer a flat-bellied cheerleader, her caesarian scar a memorial to lost motherhood, but the breasts still fended off gravity and the hips flared only an extra inch from a slender waist.

She dabbed Charlie behind her knees, in the hollow of her neck, and stepped into a midnight bikini. No bra. Tonight she'd wear something cuddly, welcoming, not too seductive. Charcoal turtleneck, plum sweater, Levi's, boots, pea coat.

Lynn went into the bedroom and picked up the newspaper on the dresser to read the personal circled in lipstick. Her heart jumped into double-time.

PO'd at MEG
Go play with someone else.

The sight of him at the airport confirmed what she had seen at Rocky Point Restaurant — Mel Gibson incarnate. Tall, strong, a rugged, almost-handsome face, dark hair curled at the nape of his neck. He did a poor job of looking relaxed, the grim set of his mouth, brooding nut-brown eyes that masked an unfathomable intensity. Was it anger she saw? Intuition told Lynn that this man had to be taken care of, once and for all.

She took a last glance in the mirror. Definitely Meg Ryan, certainly a better actress. The idea of finding a movie agent flitted in, flitted out. Stay with the quest.

I'M NOT PLAYING.
Morgan's Coffee House.
Friday at eleven.

Buck walked into Morgan's at 10:50, his hair dripping, jacket soaked. He cursed the weather, the job, the butthead supervisor who kept him late. Why even be here?

This whole thing is out of whack, he thought, a waste of time, Meg writing the script. His intestines tied into a hard knot. Too soon, too soon.

A loud murmur, like the buzz of machinery, filled the room. He sized up the Friday crowd — locals grouped in conversation, newcomers, loners. Women running the gamut from cute nymphs carded at the door to past-forties hoping to get lucky. Men, predators, dressed in everything from Costco to Land's End.

Buck took the only empty stool and ordered a Corona. He dragged from the bottle and searched for Meg. The longer he waited the more he experienced embarrassed hostility, like he'd been stood up, and the harder he stared at the entrance.

Meg came in.

Lynn took off the parka and limp rain hat, fluffed her hair and surveyed the room. Her contact lens had never been all that good, blurry at best, but she was able to make out what seemed to be a brown flight jacket at the bar.

Her heart tap-danced. Oh God, this is so high school.

Meg Ryan. And more. He noticed male customers locking onto this new arrival, sizing her up, muttering comments under their breath. She slid among them as if she were invisible. She's cool, he thought, very cool, exciting, the liquid way she flowed past the creeps, sure of herself, unafraid. Buck felt his jaw clench with a surge of unexpected jealousy. Libidinous pricks.

Jesus, she's the one.

Lynn maneuvered among the tables, eyes straight ahead, chin high, aware of the ogling pack sweating and pawing the floor, like wild animals in rut. Assholes, she thought.

She stepped up to the bar and faced the brown jacket. His eyes were milk chocolate.

"Hello," she said.

"Meg" his voice softer than she expected.

Before Lynn could respond he stood and offered his seat.

Yes, manners. He pushed in next to her, their arms touched. His warmth traveled through her sweater, immediate, disturbing.

Lynn signaled the bartender. "Haig and Haig, rocks," then to Buck, "I'm sorry about that airport thing. I was there and saw you. A secret peek. I didn't have the nerve to come up to you. Then I had to run to catch SkyWest for L.A.X."

She gave the man with Hershey Bar eyes a smile. She didn't get one back.

"Whatever," he said.

He really is hard to get. God, what a rush.

Her scotch came and he laid some bills on the bar. She shoved them back at him and gave the bartender a ten. Buck thought, don't tread on me.

There was more to it though. He guessed her paying was a way to slap him alongside the head, to make certain he knows who's in charge. Whatever was being acted out here, he wished he knew the rules.

She took his hand, gave it a firm squeeze, her green-brown eyes frank, inquisitive. "Lynnette Jennings Ward — Lynn."

"Richard Buckley Keller — Buck." He squeezed back. Her hand was hot, a firebrand.

"Hello, Richard Buckley Keller." She withdrew her fingers and held his gaze while she sipped her scotch.

Please God, don't let her be part of a nightmare.

Lynn liked the way Buck held the door for her while she slid behind the wheel. He leaned in. Light danced off the raindrops on his raven hair, his smile disarmed her.

He said, "Coffee Monday?"

"I'm not sure..."

"Starbucks, Alvarado Street, ten o'clock." Before she could protest, he let the door swing shut and moved away. She drove off, feeling his eyes on her.

Two drinks, no invasion of privacy, no come-on, no awkward insistence on following her home. He never mentioned Saturday or Sunday. Lynn had hoped for some kind of invitation for the weekend. So she could say no. Just coffee on Monday. So why give a damn? But she did give a damn. She contemplated Cannery Row slipping past the car window, light bouncing off wet pavement in stark contrast to the murky buildings. The gloom pulled at her.

By the time Lynn parked in front of her cottage the downpour had quit. She walked up the stone path. Fog ghosted to the ground, the earth her only reality. Pictures of her father jumped out of the shadows: the two of them together, playing, confiding, joyous hugging. Then dark betrayal, guilt-ridden loneliness. Tears burned her cheeks.

Lynn ran up the porch steps, dug into her pocket for the keys, entered and slammed the door. She fought to breathe, listening to the loud thump of her wounded heart, and burst into uncontrolled sobs.

They huddled at a corner table, immersed in coffee, croissants and conversation, oblivious to the deli's clamor.

"UPS warehouse, nights. Only way I have time to write," studying her. This morning her eyes were pure olive. Beautiful. Lynn Ward is frigging beautiful. He said, "A Harlequin romance every month isn't me, just makes for good, steady cash flow."

He listened to himself, all at once realizing she had maneuvered him into telling stuff too intimate, too soon. His instinct said shut up, but he couldn't. She was in charge.

"What is you, Buck Keller? Never married, what else?"

"Greece. Going to live there, write the ultimate tragedy. False resurrection, death's retribution." Make his mother the whore die, and die, and die.

She said, "University of Missouri, Wichita, Pacific Grove, Greece. Nice itinerary." Her tiny smile made his skin crawl.

"Aw hell, I'll end up in the Ozarks. Close to my pain, close to a pair of ancient foster parents." For a second Buck saw the Bible-pounding, Hitler-loving couple, drab shapes in a melancholy, deformed world. His stomach did a flip-flop.

Lynn mouthed a quiet, "Oh." He caught it—she didn't want to hear his sad tale.

"Okay, Lynnette Jennings Ward. Who, what, where?" Buck asked it with forced levity. But he was flat-out serious, had to know her, all of her.

Without answering, Lynn stood and took the coffee mugs to the counter. Jesus, he thought, she even walks beautiful, hips moving in those jeans like a Parisian runway model. She refilled the mugs and brought them back.

He got to his feet, held her chair and said, "Thanks."

Lynn liked Buck's easy manners, they complimented her. Yet she could see this interplay had ambled its way to a new plateau. It scared her. No more games, straight talk.

"Oklahoma State, philosophy," she said, "Married Roger senior year, stayed at home while he pissed away my inheritance on shitty real estate." A sorrowful loathing stirred within, for her father and his money, for the vile man who lost it. She took a huge gulp of Java Mocha to wash down the bitter recollections. All it did was burn her tongue. "Then husband disappears, gone in the night, never surfaces." He'd better not, not back to the living. Not him, or Aaron, or any of them.

"Lousy," he said, sounding sincere. It warmed her.

"I was finished with men," wished she hadn't said it, "Needed to get far away. Got my degree, joined United as a flight attendant, the great escape, never looked back." That's a lie. She never stopped looking back.

Lynn had the uneasy feeling that Buck already knew her more than any of the pain-in-the-ass shrinks, that he could actually read her mind. Buck Keller. Be careful. She hoped her goose bumps didn't show.

Buck put the Power Mac to sleep and stared over Monterey Bay's slate waters, his gaze coming to rest on the far shore. He shifted his brain into neutral, a morning ritual, a time for new ideas, to find answers to unresolved story questions. But mental snapshots of Lynn crowded in and brushed the writing aside.

Her presence in his life had become an enigma; thoughts of her raised the hair on his neck. He tried to imagine where she lived. How did her nest compare with his third floor, peek-of-the-bay walk-up? Buck stood and walked to a corkboard pinned with notes, tear sheets, articles. He ran his finger over a scrap of paper. Lynn's phone number.

Lynn. Planted as solid in his psyche as the Holy Ghost and Star Spangled Banner. Buck knew with visceral certainty that Lynn was no accident, in some bizarre way they had happened to each other. The notion wadded his gut into a tight knot.

Buck never selected any of them, at least not at a conscious level. They materialized, before the chanting began. Blurred encounters. No patterns, no rational provocations. San Mateo, Santa Cruz, Las Vegas. After all, Buck was no serial killer. He never intended to hurt them, only wanted a friend, someone to help him escape the fearful incantation.

Now Lynn was insinuating herself into his life, making his blood run hot while dread scraped across his nerves like coarse sandpaper. Buck felt the ground slipping out from under him.

Lynn dropped her coat on the bed, stepped out of her wet shoes and punched the answering machine. Her mother said it was raining in Tulsa, the psychiatrist's office wanted to confirm her appointment. And Buck.

"So how was Philadelphia? Call me."

His low voice seared her innards like a shot of Remy Martin. She put her hand to her throat, recalling the Starbucks tête-a-tête, his coolness, his damnable cocksure attitude, his subtle kiss as they stood on Alvarado Street.

She flipped through her address book, picked up the phone, hesitated, then replaced it. In command, she thought, keep it that way.

Better call the psychiatrist. Memories popped in. The trial, a ruling of self-defense, the court order, medical experts. All of it garbage. He deserved it, like Roger, like the others. She had done the right thing. Her capital punishment had been an endless battery of shrinks — smug, omnipotent, coaxing from her the one-dimensional, groveling dialogue, the mea culpa. And the medicine, its morose side effects. She hated it, hated them. Damn it all. She picked up the phone.

Naked and grotesque, the creature a phantasm of red, green, purple, its nipples charcoal. He felt his chest crushed by wriggling tentacles as he sank in a vat of syrup-sweet blood. The world spun, filled with cacophonous music. He grabbed the creature's throat and squeezed. She grinned and cackled.

Buck bolted upright, his heart thudding, his chest and face slick with sweat. Morning sun splashed across the bed, scorching his eyes. God damn her...God damn her.

He struggled out of bed. After a quick bathroom trip he nuked some of yesterday's coffee in the microwave and lifted the cup with shaking hands. He breathed the steam to hide the sour stench of his body. The telephone jangled.

Buck went to the computer table, lifted the receiver. A warning thrill ran up his backbone.

"Hello."

"All right, Richard Buckley Keller, I'll make the move," throaty, different. "I have four days. What do we do with it?"

Hang up. Run. Jesus, run.

Buck threw Lynn's duffel in the back and closed the passenger door, then eased behind the wheel of the Super Beetle. He examined her through his Ray Bans. Today her eyes were burnished emeralds and she wore all black, like a black widow. Wouldn't be surprised if she has a red patch on her belly. God, she is knockout gorgeous.

He switched on the ignition, the engine came to life. The cylinders' clamor overrode the incessant droning in his brain. No, he thought, this will be different. Not this time.

"So where do we start this incredible odyssey, Miss?"

Head back, eyes closed, she smiled and said, "Where we met, dear man. Or at least sort of met...Rocky Point Restaurant. After that, a weekend of hot baths at Esalen."

Lynn pressed her neck against the seat. Over the blur of the bridge's concrete railing she watched the crashing surf hundreds of feet below, the lapis waters beyond. She shut her eyes and jumped, arms outstretched in resplendent freedom, falling, falling. Buck's words caught her before she hit the water.

"...could be the start of a whole new thing. The ultimate personals experience."

Lynn opened her eyes and looked at him. She saw the corners of his mouth turn up in a quiet grin. Damn, he's so cocky. She was glad she hadn't taken any of the foul medicine, her mind was clear, she knew what she had to do.

She smiled. "I hope you're right."

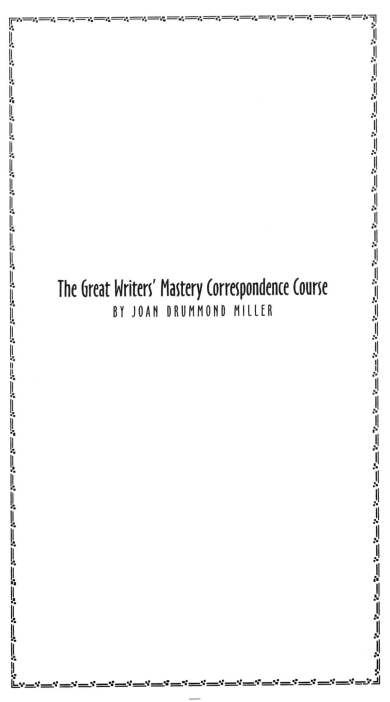

The Great Writers' Mastery Correspondence Course
BY JOAN DRUMMOND MILLER

The Great Writers' Mastery Correspondence Course
BY JOAN DRUMMOND MILLER

I lived for forty years on the Monterey Peninsula thinking I was a screw-up until one day I realized I was a writer. Kids used to say I was charming so I started in sales, but it just didn't go anywhere. Then I tried acting. I knew I was good but I never could make it from community theater to any kind of paying job.

One morning I looked into my breakfast coffee and saw the truth. I said to Ma, "I'm a screw-up, livin' at home. Bringin' in damned near no money. I never have a decent job."

"Don't worry, son," she said, "It's a shame to rush yourself. You just haven't met up with your destiny yet."

The next day it happened. Just like Ma said it would. I was out in the hammock reading *Sweet Thursday*, that's by John Steinbeck, and I remembered he had pretty much been a screw-up until he realized he was a writer. If you're a writer it doesn't matter that you're bad at everything else. So I knew that's what I must be: a writer.

Ma was great. "You're destiny's arrived," she said and bought me the "Great Writers' Mastery Correspondence Course."

After three years of rejection slips, I still didn't doubt my destiny or my "Great Writers" course, but I saw the odds. They don't give you the time of day if you're just starting. Want all the big names. First-time authors can't get a break. I had more blood on every page than any of them. I knew every twisted way to kill. I used porn and horror in all my openings and still they wouldn't listen. Me and my destiny needed a new direction. So I studied Anne Rice like a textbook. This woman was really raking it in. She pretended like she was a vampire. I needed a gimmick. Trouble was she'd already snatched the best one.

For the next week I opened and closed the library looking up zombies, monsters, grave snatchers, voodoo priests and third-world terrorists. Nothing clicked. One day it came like a vision. My childhood favorite: a werewolf. *The Confessions of a Werewolf.* I got really excited. Move over, Anne Rice.

I knew the first thing I would need. I had to get a place in the wilderness. Remote, wild. A place to feel the part.

I drove down Highway One toward Big Sur. Stopped at Rocky Point Restaurant for a beer and a look at Mickey, my favorite hostess. She mentioned a cottage in the back was vacant and for rent.

When I told Ma, she was all for it. Excited. Everything I did was exciting to Ma. With a gal like Ma in your corner, you don't need to rebel. That's probably why we've stuck together.

The cottage was just right for us. None of the customers, or even the employees, could see it. It was hidden on the far side in a dark grove of cypresses. A front deck ran over the cliff and the great, raw ocean below smashed against the rocks.

For the first couple of days I climbed over the rocks and explored the caves. I was learning the underbrush, holes and hiding places. I wrote down all the creatures, but I didn't know all the birds.

This was untamed country where a werewolf would be happy. Ma was disappointed that we couldn't watch TV. Something about the mountains. Neither one of us liked music so the radio was out. I'd brought a lot of reading, had checked out all the Sherlock Holmes and werewolf books from the Monterey library.

I went into town to rent some videos for me and Ma. I got all the werewolf movies they had and ordered a couple more. I liked the earliest ones with Lon Chaney Jr. He had the perfect make-up: fangs, hair sprouting out of his cheeks and forehead and lots on top, real hairy hands with claws. The bottom half of him stayed just the same. I thought he should have had a hairy chest.

By the end of the week I got out my old stage make-up and wigs and turned myself into a great werewolf. Better than Mr. Chaney because I glued more patches of fur on my face. It was a real breakthrough.

Now when I looked in the mirror I could almost scare myself. I practiced snarls and growls and opening my mouth to show my fangs. Get inside your character, the "Great Writer's Course" said. I was on my way.

A few times I practiced moving slowly on all fours, trying on my new self. I crawled up the steep cliff outside the dining room at Rocky Point just out of sight of the hungry customers cutting their almost raw hunks of meat. I knew they couldn't see me as they looked out the windows to the sea below, but I wondered, anyhow, what they would do, and the thought was delicious. What if I just reared up in all my six-foot wolf magnificence and showed my face right up against the glass? It would make a great movie scene. Never quite had the nerve to try it out.

A guy in the kitchen loaned me some traps. I caught a sea gull and drank his blood. This was all starting to click, feel good. I was living the part. I asked Ma to buy me some fur fabric and she made me a jacket that was really wolfish. I bought some leather gloves. She sewed fur on them, and claws. Ma wanted to get me a mask but I didn't want one. I liked to do my own make-up.

One night there was a full moon. I put on my outfit and prowled the hills feeling my destiny calling. When coyotes howled, I answered back. I hid in the brush (usually on all fours) and when raccoons and opossums came near, I jumped out to catch them, but they were too fast. I kept the traps.

A week later, after midnight, I wandered over to the other side to the Rocky Point parking lot. Through the window I saw David, the bartender, an old woman in the corner drinking beer, and a couple of young guys standing at the bar. Nobody else in the place. Might be fun to show off my outfit. I opened the sliding door and lunged forward, growling.

"What the hell...?" one of the guys yelled. At first, they looked startled, then they went back to their conversation and ignored me.

I went over to the old lady and snuffled my snout at her pretzels. She put my head in her lap, petted my forehead, the top of my head. She put some pretzels in my mouth. A good ol' gal. She reminded me of Ma.

"Get the hell outta here" cut through the air. "We don't serve no monsters." Then David laughed.

Blood beat in my head. Waves of hatred. I thought about attack. That would wipe the stupid grin off his face fast if I clawed his throat bloody. Shit! Those young guys would jump me. Get a grip. I turned and got out of there fast. But I was different, dangerously free, when I had on my werewolf suit.

I worked at being my old self for the next couple days. I wrote all the time, slept little. I was on fire. I knew it was good. The werewolf spoke through me and I was his voice. This was just what they recommended. What the greats talked about. "Let the character possess you," said the "Great Writer's Correspondence Course."

I didn't put on the suit. I was too tired to roam the hills. The coyotes were lonely as I slept the sleep of a happy man who sees his destiny arrive. Maybe I was also a little scared of the suit.

The only breaks I gave myself were mid-afternoon snacks. I'd get all slicked up and go over to Rocky Point Restaurant to see Mickey and devour a beer, some calamari and cheese bread. The truth is I was quite smitten with Mickey: so tiny, amusing and blonde. I was sure she liked me. When I opened the front door she always wrapped me in a smile. Not just with her mouth, but her eyes, too.

The big day came. I mailed the first forty pages and a plot synopsis and marked my calendar. I was prepared to wait for a month or two. That's what the "Great Writer's" manual said, "Be prepared to wait a month or two."

Surprise! On the next Wednesday, Mickey came over to the cottage.

"There's someone on the desk phone who wants to talk to you." She was cute with her eyes open wide. She was surprised. "Says it's urgent."

"Hello," I said.

"It's great," a deep voice said, "Really nutty; weird, tension-loaded backstory. The best part's that I can feel the underlying violence though nothing terrible has happened yet."

It was beginning to sink in on me. He liked it. He really did!

"My name's Richard Selva. I'm the literary scout for Bixby Books. If the rest of it is as good as this we'll send out our standard contract. It is finished, right?"

"Yes," I lied.

"Great! I want it yesterday."

"It still needs a few revisions," I lied again.

"All right. Mail it to me next week. This could be really big."

"What is it?" Mickey asked, still waiting by the phone, but I didn't answer.

I stumbled back to the cabin, my mind and feet not in the same place. I had made it. No more screw-ups. Respect. Fame.

I'd be somebody with his picture on a back cover. The big time. I was proud. Nervous, too. I had to write two hundred pages in a week.

Didn't tell Ma. After she was in bed, I went to my room to undress. I opened the closet to hang up my pants. I saw my werewolf suit.

Once inside it I felt better. By the time my make-up was on, I was calmer. I sat at the computer and started to write. Then I took out a pad and got on the floor. I was more comfortable crouching. Later, I stretched out and fell asleep.

After I cleaned up for breakfast I went back to the computer, prepared to begin my adventure.

The first ten minutes I waited expectantly. The next thirty were agony. No words. Finally I wrote, "Every good boy does fine." Terror. I would not be a screw-up. No way. Writer's block wouldn't steal my destiny.

I had calamari and exchanged jokes with Mickey. When I got home, I sat at the computer again. Nothing. Now I was depressed. Only one thing to do: sleep.

Woke from my nap with the answer, went right into my room and put on the suit, my make-up. Ma wasn't back from town yet. It was just starting to get dark. Didn't turn on any lights. Just prowled around. Saw myself in the mirror. Took comfort in my half-light reflection.

I wandered out into the coming night, not toward the restaurant but to the woods. Tonight I wanted no contact with the human race.

To be not human is like opening some door in a dark room and walking out. I was no longer interested in Rudolf Ottermeyer, screw-up; I was beyond human responsibilities, human cares. Inside the wolf, I was unafraid. Strong. At last, a mindless, wild creature.

I wrote fifty pages non-stop and finally slept. Even in my sleep the wolf possessed me. I dreamed of Mickey. Sex, of course. Only I was the wolf fawning on her, rubbing my shaggy head against her tiny, warm breasts, smelling her intense sweetness.

All week I wore the suit, wrote all day like a beast possessed, wandered deep in the woods for an hour or so before sleep, dreamed again of pawing Mickey. I no longer enjoyed killing the entrapped birds and immediately drinking their blood, like in the early days. I could grow strangely sexually aroused by holding the newly-killed prey in my mouth and loping slowly through the woods. It felt even better than the nightly dreams of Mickey.

As my plot came to a climax, I became obsessed. I didn't bother to sleep at night. I wrote all the time. When I was too tired to see, I dropped by my computer and caught an hour or two. I lived in my wolf suit all the time. I couldn't tell day from night, beast from author. Hadn't been out for calamari in days, lived on stale crackers and canned soup.

At last a hundred sixty pages. A little short. I didn't care. I had no more. It was over.

Good ol' Ma took my manuscript into Carmel so she could get it out express mail. She told me how proud she was I found destiny. She was staying overnight in town. Needed some medical tests.

I crawled into the bed I hadn't seen all week and slept for I don't know how long. I was too tired to even take off the wolf suit. A light shattered my dark and split my head. Ruined my favorite sex dream. I tried to focus. All I could see was white fur.

Then I heard the voice. There was only one voice like that. I grabbed Mickey, pulled her onto the bed and lay on top of her.

I tore open the furry coat. Searched for her tiny bare breasts to rest my shaggy head on. Dreams really come true when you are a successful author and not some stupid screw-up.

I felt her struggle, heard her screams. I lowered my head and bit a hole in her neck. Blood everywhere. Red on white fur. Heard her loud, gasping breath.

I don't have much I can remember after that. I'm caged now and they won't let me wear my suit. I'm lonely for Ma, the coyotes and the wild hills of Big Sur.

I'm a success, though. Richard Selva says all the publicity put my book over the top. This week we made the New York Times best seller list. I owe it all to "The Great Writers' Mastery Correspondence Course."

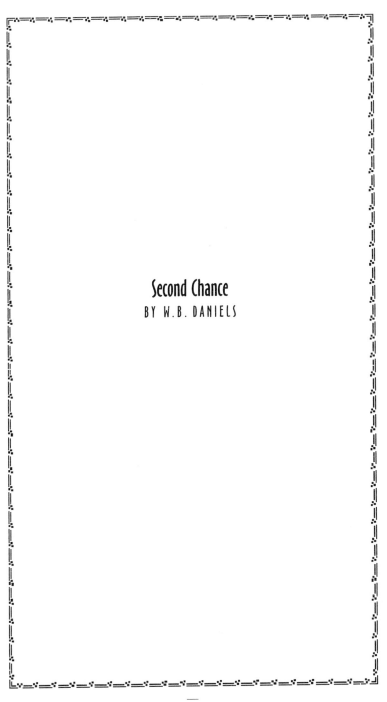

Second Chance
BY W.B. DANIELS

Second Chance
BY W.B. DANIELS

As she sits by the window at the Rocky Point Restaurant about to order a lunch she won't eat, from a menu she despises, it occurs to Mildred Donnelly that her son, Dewey, is a fool to trust her. That does not surprise Mildred. She believes most men are fools, including the nervous, nearly bald, young lawyer opposite her, Jeffrey Miles, who Dewey hired to draw the will Mildred plans to revoke as soon as she gets what she wants. "Is it certified, Mr. Miles? It has to be certified," Mildred says.

"I'm sure it's certified, Mrs. Donnelly. It was here a minute ago," Miles says while searching his file.

"We're not going through with this unless it's certified. If it's not just the way I want it, you both can take all your papers and go away."

"Don't be impatient, Mother," says Dewey. "It's going to be the way you want it."

"Then why is it taking him so long to find it?"

A band of sweat blooms on Miles' forehead. "I'm doing the best I can."

"Where did you find this lawyer, Dewey?"

"Yellow pages," Dewey says. "His ad said, 'No Frill Wills, $125.'"

"I should have known."

"Here it is," Miles says, relieved. "See, Ms. Donnelly, it says right here that you've adopted April."

"Thank God. Now the poor child has a chance," says Mildred. "That bitch is finally out of her life."

"Well, that bitch, as you say, is still April's guardian if you and I die, Mother."

"I don't like that," Mildred says. "You both can go to hell if you think I'll tolerate April continuing a relationship with that trash."

Mildred watches Dewey's worried insipid face make an effort to be diplomatic with her. She knows he wants to remind her that he had told her about his wife, Janet's, insistence that she remain as April's guardian if Mildred and Dewey were gone. It was the only condition Janet imposed for her consent to April's adoption. Mildred wants Dewey to believe that she has forgotten that discussion, has become bitchy and difficult, and requires his total concentration to bring her back on track. Being difficult is a power game Mildred loves to play. Their meeting would be no fun unless she ruined their lunch.

As Dewey begins his diplomatic effort with an unimaginative, "But mother..," Mildred interrupts by saying to Jeffrey Miles, "You're probably wondering where I got this big rock." Mildred fingers the large diamond on her left hand. Mildred loves segues because they oblige listeners who want something to be attentive.

"It's very lovely," says Jeffrey Miles.

"Of course it's lovely. Doing no frill wills, you'll never be this close to anything so lovely again in your life." Mildred watches Miles swallow the insult. "Dewey's daddy gave it to me when we married. He thought it would make me feel like a star again. I was almost a star, you know, until my career was stolen." She takes off her large round sunglasses that cover a thick scar running from her right eyebrow through her eyelid and down to her nostril. "This, Mr. Miles, brought Dewey into this world. I'd never have married Harold Donnelly or had a child if that drunk hadn't jumped the divider on the Pasadena Freeway. I was at the height of my career in TV commercials. Of course, they were just the beginning. My agent was getting me readings for serious parts. Suddenly, all that came to an end."

This is where Mildred usually pauses. A listener needs a moment to digest her disfigurement. She throws her head back in the gesture her acting coach said displayed courage and strength. She looks reflectively at the surf crashing on the rocks below the restaurant window for six beats and then swallows most of the flute of champagne that has been waiting by her left hand. Pointing to the keloid, she says, "Dewey owes his life to this, don't you, Dewey?"

"How many times do I have to listen to that?"

"I'm sure Mr. Miles is interested, aren't you, Mr. Miles?"

"Of course," says the lawyer.

Mildred knows the moment has come for her widow's speech. "Harold Donnelly was such a dear." On cue her eyes begin to fill. "He bought me whatever I wanted to get me out of my depression, to revive me. He built my beautiful house here at Kasler Point. He said if I didn't live near Hollywood, I'd forget that it wasn't my town anymore. Harold was the only one I would consider. Women like me and Jackie O. require husbands who can afford high maintenance. We still own big chunks of Beverly Hills."

"What does Mr. Donelly do?"

"Do? Why Mr. Donnelly doesn't do anything. He's dead," Mildred says, as if she is surprised at Jeffrey's ignorance.

"I'm sorry," says Miles.

"Don't be sorry. It's Dewey's fault."

"Mother, stop."

"No. Your lawyer should know what you did."

Mildred is amused with the puzzlement on Miles' face. "Tell him, Dewey. Tell him how you killed your father."

If Dewey complies, Mildred expects him to talk about the ground floor room with the sliding glass doors that open onto the windy deck above the surf where Harold spent most of his days assembling model airplanes. After nearly a decade, it was filled with a squadron of remote-controlled miniature aircraft. Each plane was the same. Harold's ambition was to fly all his models at once as if they were taking off to bomb London. Harold had an attraction for the Third Reich.

Dewey had complained that his father's obsession with his Luffwaffe squadron was no fun. He wouldn't let Dewey build a single model. Dewey's work had to be authentic in every detail before Harold Donnelly would let it leave "his factory." Mildred ignored Dewey's complaints.

When Dewey learned that other kids' dads flew real airplanes, he challenged Harold to fly. Harold bought a plane and hired pilots to fly it back and forth over the Monterey Airport. Dewey said that was more boring than watching Harold work on his squadron. To prove himself a man, Harold took flying lessons. On his first solo flight, he under-shot the runway.

"Go ahead, Dewey. Tell Mr. Miles."

"I won't."

Insisting further felt like a bore. Mildred moved on. "Actually, Harold's passing was a blessing. It gave me the chance to be with some real men, young men, men who can love a sexually experienced woman. I could never allow them to stay too long. I had to protect my growing son. And I made some mistakes, like leaving Dewey with Lucien that summer I took my spiritual journey to India with Sean."

Mildred still refused to read the reports of the admitting psychologist at "that special school" Dewey attended after he went out of control at Carmel High the next year. She was confident the genes Dewey got from Harold were responsible for his need for shock therapy and regular medication. "Harold's death is ancient history now, isn't it, Dewey?" she said. "We're here to do something wonderful about April's future, aren't we? Today April gets a clean slate, a second chance. So tell me, Mr. Miles, does the certified paper say I am in charge of April's life?"

Jeffrey Miles pushes a paper from his file in front of Mildred. "It says that you have adopted April; you're April's mother. So it's just like Dewey's daughter is Dewey's sister."

"Mother sounds better than grandmother. Grandmother sounds ugly and old. I certainly like that part, Mr. Miles."

"There's more. Because both Dewey and April are now your children, they will inherit equally from you in the event of your death."

"What if April meets with an unfortunate accident?" Mildred says.

"Then everything goes to Dewey."

"I don't like that. It creates dangerous incentives for Dewey."

Miles looks at her with mild exasperation. "There are no dangerous incentives, Mrs. Donnelly. If a beneficiary murders the testator, he gets nothing under the law. The more likely scenario is that April will survive both of you and receive all of your estate."

"If there is any left," Mildred says. "I'm a big spender."

Jeffrey smiles. "If there are no assets left, of course there will be nothing for April."

"And I can do whatever I want with April?"

"You are obliged to support her and care for her."

"She will have every advantage. And there will be no interference from her mother?"

"She has no more say in April's life."

"I will be the only influence on her life?"

"You can look at it that way, Mrs. Donnelly."

"Where are April's things?" Mildred asks.

"Right here," says Dewey.

"Dewey, tell our waitress to bring us a garbage bag."

The guest tables at Rocky Point extend into the dining room like fingers from the glassed wall facing the ocean. At the unoccupied end of their table, Jeffrey Miles opens a small battered suitcase and waits for Dewey to return with a garbage bag.

"April has not seen this, of course?" Mildred says.

"Mother, these are her belongings. Of course she's seen them before. All we told April is that she is going to stay at grandma's house for a while. Janet is going to drop her off at your house today at four."

"Open it," Mildred says.

"Do we need to do this, Mother?"

"I don't want any sentimental trash cluttering April's new life. That's why we're doing this. I would think, Dewey, you would have the brains to understand that."

April's clothes are neatly packed. On the top, under the strap, Mildred sees an envelope with "April" written on it in large cursive letters. "Oh God, not a wimpy farewell note. Give it to me, Mr. Miles."

Mildred rips open the envelope. Her eyes scan the text. "I wonder how many drafts it took her to write this?" she asks. The note tells April she is going to live with her grandmother.

Mommy and Daddy want what's best for you. Grandma Mildred can give you so much more than we can. You will go to a new school that will start you on the road to college so you can grow up to be an important person, not a common and ordinary one like your mommy. But you should always know, no matter what you do, April, your mommy loves you.

"Well, we can't have this around," Mildred says as she tears the letter up. "What else is in there?"

"You'd better let me, Jeff," Dewey says.

After they trade places to give Dewey better access to the suitcase, Dewey unties the strap securing the contents. The first is a thin wool blanket.

"What's that God-awful thing?"

"This is April's 'blanky'." Dewey says. "She sleeps with it every night."

"Not any more," says Mildred. "Toss it." Dewey unfolds the garbage bag and puts April's blanky inside.

"What else?" Mildred asks.

One by one Mildred rejects the contents of April's suitcase and Dewey places them in the garbage bag, until all that is left is a white leatherette covered Bible. Inside, on the first page, it reads, "Presented to April Donnelly by the Primary Department of the South Fresno Community Presbyterian Church School, 12th June 1998."

As he closes the cover, Dewey begins to cry. "I don't want you to throw this away."

Mildred knows she may have reached Dewey's point of resistance. If she goes too far, he might climb on some irrational high horse and ruin her plans. "April can keep the Bible, Dewey. Now I want a real drink," she says.

Mildred downs her Old Fashioned and says, "So the burdens of motherhood are upon me once again. I hope you appreciate what I am doing for you and for April. It's not every parent who would make the sacrifices I am making. What then do I need to do, Mr. Miles?"

"We need to get two of the waitresses to act as witnesses to your will. I have arranged that."

"And then?"

"I give you your certified copy of the order of the court by which you adopted April as you and Dewey have agreed. Then I take the original will back to my office, put it in my safe, and send you copies for your files."

Mildred notes Dewey's face is again suspenseful and expectant. She has run out of ideas of how to humiliate him further. She reminds herself that she really is doing something wonderful for Dewey. His psychological problems prevent him from ever being regularly employed. What could Janet ever amount to as a waitress? Yes, Mildred tells herself, she is making a magnanimous sacrifice for the betterment of the next generation. Besides, if she doesn't like April, she'll send her home and revoke the will. Getting out of the commitment will be just as easy as getting into it. "All right," says Mildred, "Call the witnesses. Let's get this boring lunch over with so I can go meet my daughter."

After Dewey and Mildred say goodbye to Jeffrey Miles, they walk to Mildred's red and gray Rolls Royce.

"I'll drive," says Dewey. "You've had three Old Fashioneds."

"I have the right to celebrate." Mildred hands him the keys.

The driveway from the parking lot at Rocky Point Restaurant twists up for an eighth of a mile to Highway One. With the buzz of the booze and the self-satisfaction that she has performed well, Mildred relaxes into the deep leather back seat of the Rolls. She expects Dewey to turn left on Highway One and drive two miles to the electric gate at her driveway above Kasler Point. Mildred plans to nap for an hour, take a long bath, and change clothes to prepare for April's arrival at four. She closes her eyes and contemplates the second motherhood chapter of her life.

Mildred is roused from her musing by the sense that Dewey has turned right instead of left.

"What are you doing?" Mildred says.

"Taking a little drive, Mother. We have time to kill until four."

"I do not want to kill time with you, Dewey. Take me home at once."

"Sure, Mom."

Mildred closes her eyes again. She assumes that the acceleration of the Rolls is a symptom of Dewey's anger at her rejection of his invitation. She has nothing more to say to him. As far as she is concerned, if she never sees Dewey again, that will be just fine.

Mildred opens her eyes when she senses something is wrong. The Rolls is speeding toward the corner north of Bixby Bridge. Instead of turning, Dewey drives straight. Mildred lunges toward Dewey's pimpled neck with her long manicured nails. Without a guard rail the Rolls maintains its speed off the three hundred foot cliff. Mildred sees sky, rocks, and then surf. The last thing she hears is Dewey screaming, "Yippee ki yea, bitch!"

On The Rocks
BY MAGGIE HARDY

On The Rocks
BY MAGGIE HARDY

The singing telegram arrived at their table without warning.

A young woman in a scant outfit and a Betty Boop mask sang *I want to be loved by you and nobody else but you* as she boo-boo-be-dooped her way into Ted's lap.

She planted a wet one on his lips and announced to all of Rocky Point Restaurant that it was from "your only true love."

The crowd applauded. Ted turned beet red and pushed the singer up and away from him. Julie, stunned, sat motionless.

The man at the next table reached over to congratulate Ted. A low long whistle followed Betty Boop as she scampered out of the restaurant, blowing kisses to the diners.

Ted sputtered as he tried to regain his composure. "Great engagement present, Jules."

Julie folded her arms tight against her chest. "It's not from me."

Wilhelm, the maitre d', brought a small envelope to the table. "Miss Boop left this for you." He handed Ted a small white envelope marked *To My Darling*. Ted pushed it into his pocket.

"Open it," Julie said in a cold hard voice.

"If it's not from you, how important can it be?"

"Open it."

Ted started to put it in his pocket again. She reached across the table. "Open it or I will."

He complied.

"Now read it aloud."

"No."

She grabbed the card from him, "I love you more than anyone or anything." Julie ripped the words into small shreds. She gulped her wine and tried to hold back her tears.

Ted reached for her hand across the white tablecloth. "Sweetheart, don't spoil tonight."

She pulled her hand away and stared out the window at the purple-streaked sky and waves crashing below. "Don't tell me you don't know that woman."

Rocky Point had always been their restaurant. They'd come here on their first date and now to celebrate their engagement.

"Say something," Ted reached for her hand again.

She continued to stare out at the endless sea. "I wish I were out there, a thousand miles from you. From her."

"It's nothing. Zip. Nada."

"You call getting a singing telegram at our restaurant from another woman, nothing?"

"Maybe it was Arnie making a joke."

"Our engagement is a joke?"

He let out a long low sigh. "No, it's the most important thing. What can I do to make it all right?"

"Which one of your bimbo girlfriends is it from?"

Ted lost his cool. "We're back to this, are we? So I've had some women in my past. So what, I'm marrying you."

"Maybe not," Julie narrowed her eyes.

They sat in silence. Her tears came fast. "This is not the first time something like this has happened."

"Geez, Jules, let it go. It was a prank. Let's watch the sunset."

Julie looked at his reflection in the window and took a long drink of wine.

"You're imagining things."

"No I'm not."

He shushed her. "Do I look like the kind of guy that women would chase to the ends of the earth?"

Julie started to smile.

"Do I?"

"You're right. Arnie is a jerk."

"No, he's a gigantic, colossal, world class jerk."

Her smile broadened. They laughed in unison and uttered "Arnie" at exactly the same time.

A calm settled over them. This time she reached for him. They sat looking out at the fading light.

Ted watched new tears streak Julie's face. "Hey, I thought we were over that."

She nodded. "We are. I love you so much. I don't want to share you with anyone." She wiped the tears with the back of her hand. "I probably look like hell."

"You look beautiful."

Julie pushed her chair from the table. She laughed. "I'll be right back."

Rummaging through her bag, she nearly knocked into a woman as she rounded the corner to the restroom. "Sorry, didn't see you."

Together they entered the small room. "No matter," said the tall blonde in leather pants. "I ran in here to use the head and clean my contact. It's driving me crazy." She plucked the lens from her eye, rinsed it and stuck it back in.

"Do you know this is the only bathroom between Big Sur and Carmel?" The woman moved into the stall and clicked the door.

"I never really thought about it." Julie looked in the mirror at the greasy black streaks on her face.

"What's with the tears?"

"It's my boyfriend. We just got engaged."

"And you're crying over that? Most girls would be thrilled."

"We had a small misunderstanding, that's all."

"Oh?"

"I was being silly, insecure." She snorted in contempt. "His last girlfriend was named Brandy. The one before that did lingerie ads." She peered at her reflection. "Then there's me."

"You look great, hon. Men can be such pigs. So inconsiderate. The love of my life got engaged. Bastard didn't dare tell me, his mother let it slip."

A flush came from behind the door and Julie didn't hear the rest of what she said.

The woman emerged. Julie threw the paper towel into the bin and took a sidelong glance at the long legs stuffed into the tight pants.

The woman turned on the faucet, "So let's see the ring. That's how you know if a man really loves you. The size of the ring."

Julie thrust out her hand.

"Whew, honey, that is a killer all right. He loves you to death."

Julie twisted the ring. "I know. Sometimes love..."

"Hurts. Boy, don't I know." With that, the blonde sucked in her stomach and headed out the door.

Alone, Julie puckered up her mouth. "I can boo-boo-be-doop with the best of them." She headed out the door and caught sight of the blonde crawling on all fours outside the front door.

"You okay?"

"Damn contact popped out of my eye again. Help me look for it."

"Ted's waiting."

"Believe me, he'll wait forever. Got a flashlight right here."

Julie hesitated and then headed toward the door, "Okay, a quick look."

Ted alternated sipping his wine and drumming his fingers on the table. Wilhelm refilled his glass.

"We're honored to have you back on such a special occasion, Mr. David."

"Thanks." He stopped drumming his fingers.

"It's the first time we've ever had a singing telegram here." Wilhelm grinned. "She was quite something."

"Julie's gone off to fix her makeup. It was a bit more than she expected."

"Ah, it always is when you're in love."

"She'll be in there an hour if I know her, adding this and blushing that."

"Women and their makeup." They laughed as Wilhelm sallied into the sea of diners.

Ted's cell phone rang, Wilhelm shot him a look. "Would you mind taking that outside."

"No problem, I've caused enough excitement for the night." Ted beelined to the door and whispered into phone, "Hey there, give me a second."

The chilly breeze whispered through the cypress. Ted pulled his jacket close and leaned against his car. "Very funny, Arnie. Julie's all pissed off." He pressed the phone closer. "Whaddaya mean, it wasn't you?"

Ted inched out of the wind and back into the restaurant. "I'll go easy on you, just fess up. Hang on." He stopped a red haired woman coming from the restroom. "Excuse me, is there a woman in there?"

The woman shook her head and moved toward the dining room.

Ted redirected his attention to his cell phone. "I've got to go. Jules has flown the coop. She's gotta be pissed at me." He paused. "Damn right, I'm the one who should be pissed."

Ted elbowed his way into the kitchen. Wilhelm stopped tallying the receipts.

"I need a flashlight, Julie's not in the bathroom or the car."

Wilhelm grabbed his emergency light. "Let's go. Benny, turn on the flood lights out back."

The two men slammed out the side door into the charcoal night. They picked their way down the path behind the restaurant and made their way toward the shadowy grove of cypress.

Nothing. They retraced their steps and cut across to the other side. They descended the staircase to the deck below.

An older couple, holding hands, were caught off guard. "My heavens, you scared the life out of us," uttered the woman.

"Have you seen a young woman down here?"

"You're the young man with the stripper, right?" asked the gray haired man.

"Dear, that wasn't a stripper. It was a singing telegram. Very romantic." His wife patted his hand.

Ted moved closer. "Have you seen her?"

"No, we've been down here for a few minutes. A little stroll and a few smooches."

"Are you sure?"

"Yes, absolutely, I am," the wife responded. "Did you have a lover's spat?"

Ted raced back up the stairs, "None of your business."

"Calm down." Wilhelm patted Ted's shoulder. "Take it easy. We'll find her."

"Let's split up. I'll go back down the path and you check over by the point." Ted started toward the dirt path without waiting for Wilhelm's answer. "Damn it, Julie, if you're looking for a fight, you got it!"

Twenty-five minutes later, still no Julie.

"Perhaps she called a friend," Jorge, the waiter, suggested as they huddled in the bar.

"No way. Julie's a drama queen. She would have demanded the keys or to be taken home." Ted reached for his cell phone and dialed Julie's number. No answer. He tried Amy's. She hadn't heard from Julie since the day before yesterday.

Wilhelm tried to keep his staff from lingering for the latest update. "My guess is she found a quiet spot and is thinking things over."

Ted banged his fist on the bar. "Damn it. We've looked everywhere."

"Hope she didn't try to bum a ride into town or walk up Highway One. Way too dark and dangerous for that," Jorge added.

Wilhelm motioned the staff back into the dining room. "I doubt that. We haven't had any diners come in or out since she disappeared." He poured a generous glass of wine for Ted.

Ted slugged it down and headed for the door. "Wait 'til I get my hands on her."

On the rocks. Face down. Spread eagled.

It was the elderly couple who spotted Julie's body. They barely caught sight of her white jacket in the moonlight. Ben, the Highway Patrol officer, arrived as the Search and Rescue Team clambered down the slippery rocks to her body. He held Ted back as Julie's body reached the ledge. Ted whispered her name over and over again as he struggled to be closer to her.

Ben considered himself the protector of Big Sur and didn't like its image tarnished any more than his badge. This could be a sticky one. Bad for business.

As they covered her body, Ted noticed Julie's engagement ring was missing.

"I'd just given it to her. Tonight was a celebration."

"Some celebration," Ben jotted in his notebook. "Ok, let's start over from the beginning. You'd had a fight."

Jimmy, his assistant, butted in, "Ben, it could be suicide, you know. Lover's quarrel. One of the guests heard the two of you fighting over another woman."

Ted shouted at the young officer. " That's not true."

Ben motioned Jimmy aside. "That's enough." Ben left Jimmy to tidy up the details with the Coroner and went inside. Ted followed. Ben cordoned off the restaurant and detained the dinner guests. "No one in or out and that includes the help." Wilhelm nodded.

Ben took Ted aside. "Okay, you had a fight. Then what?"

"She went to the ladies' room."

"I saw her go in," offered a busboy.

"See anyone else?"

"No, nobody."

Wilhelm confirmed that no one else had been around. "The only one besides the guests was the singing telegram and I saw her leave. Julie was still at the table."

"Could have waited for her, ever think about that?" Ben grumbled.

Ted twisted a bar napkin into a tight wad. "She'd have no way of knowing Julie was going to leave the table."

Ben addressed the elderly couple. Did you see anyone out there?"

"No," the wife warbled.

Her husband reinforced her answer. "We were on our way to the car and walked to the edge to take one last look at the sea. We're from Michigan and don't have an ocean, you know."

"Right." He addressed the diners." Okay, for the last time, did anyone see or hear anything out of the ordinary?"

From the back of the bar area, a hand shot up. A young man spoke, "I saw a shadow over by the gazebo."

"Shut up, Bill. We'll be here all night," his wife answered.

"Are you certain?" Ben flipped the page of his notepad.

"Maybe not. It might have been a waiter's reflection in the window."

"Next?" Ben stood up and adjusted the waistband of his uniform.

Another hour passed before Ben finished his interrogations. When he was done, he let each one go with instructions. "If you think of anything, you call. Understand?"

Exhaustion settled on Ted's face, his eyes red but dry.

Ben cleared the room of everyone except him. "Wilhelm said you were visibly upset with your fiancee."

"Are you saying, I might have...."

"Well?"

"That's absurd," Ted shot back.

Ben shifted his weight. "Okay, then, do you think Ms. Washburn would have any reason to kill herself?"

"Look, her engagement ring is missing. Doesn't that mean anything? Like robbery? Murder?"

"Bear with me, sir."

"Damn it. My fiancee has been murdered over a crummy ring."

Ben stared intently at Ted. " Or perhaps you were..."

They were interrupted by Wilhelm and one of the sous chefs. Wilhelm pushed Ralph forward. "Tell them what you saw."

Ralph hesitated, "I don't want to get anyone in trouble."

"Just tell the truth," Ben admonished.

"Well, I was out having a smoke and Barnacle Bill was out there, rummaging through the garbage.

Wilhelm shook his head. "Damn, I've told him not to do that. Christ, there's a shelter in Monterey."

Ralph jumped in. "Bill doesn't want to live in a shelter. He likes freestyling it out here along the coast."

"Did you talk with him?"

"Yes."

"And?"

I gave him a loaf of bread." Ralph shot Wilhelm a look. "Sorry."

Wilhelm patted him on the shoulder, "I've done the same thing."

Ben let out a long, low sigh. "Can we get back to Bill?" He turned to Wilhelm. "Do you think you could round him up for questioning?"

"We'd have to find him first. Probably half way to Ragged Point by now. Even if we did, he's pretty damn squirrely."

Ralph spoke up. "There's no way Bill would hurt anyone. He's harmless."

"That's what they said about the Hillside Slayer. Try and find him for me, okay, son?"

Ben took a step closer to Ted. "If you didn't do it, and she didn't do it, do you know anyone who might wish to do Ms. Washburn any harm?"

"Everyone adored her."

"Even you?"

"Yes. Yes. Yes. We were going to be married."

"Maybe you changed your mind, maybe she changed hers. Things happen."

Jimmy hustled into the bar. "I've checked the phone book and information, sir, there isn't one singing telegram company in all of Monterey County."

Ben rubbed the back of his neck. "Figures. Mr. David we'll need you to come into the morgue to officially identify Ms. Washburn's body."

He slammed his notebook shut. "Jimmy, tell everyone to go home and put up the yellow tape. We're locking the place up 'til the investigators go through in the daylight. Who knows what they might find." He turned to Ted. "They might even find that ring you're so worried about."

Wilhelm moaned. "What about business? The employees? The fresh fish in the fridge?"

"It's a crime scene, buddy. I'll have Jimmy call you tomorrow. For now, everybody out. Jimmy, tell Charlie to patrol the grounds every fifteen minutes in case anyone tries to come back."

"Right, boss."

"Mr. David, I want you to do some hard thinking. Search your soul, see if there's anything you want to tell me."

Ted flared. "What about that Bill guy, the old couple?"

Ben shrugged his shoulders. "Maybe she was worried you didn't really love her. Hated herself for saying yes in the first place. Took the easy way out."

"No! It wasn't suicide. She wouldn't. Couldn't."

"Don't be so fast to judge, Mr. David. That way you'd be in the clear."

Ben waited until the last car had crawled up the steep drive. "Damn, why did this have to happen on my watch."

He slammed the door of his patrol car and followed Ted's car onto Highway One. He tailed him all the way into Carmel. When Ted turned down Ocean Avenue, Ben let him slowly trail out of sight. "Poor bastard. Either way his life is crap."

The tall blonde cinched her leather jacket tight against the wind and rubbed the diamond ring against her sleeve. She tossed the cheap costume and black wig into the dumpster behind Safeway, walked to the pay phone and dialed.

When she reached the answering machine, she whispered, "Hi Teddy darling, it's Brandy. I'm back in town and was wondering if we could get together."

Little Blue Jewels
BY NEIL HUNTER

Little Blue Jewels
BY NEIL HUNTER

"I got a strange feeling about this, Zip," Sheriff Tanner Sims mumbled. It nagged him, a phantom itch he couldn't scratch, like the one in the middle of his spine from disc surgery three years ago. He and Deputy Zip Hessler walked to where they'd parked the car at Rocky Point Restaurant. The popular, isolated dining spot sat perched on a cliff over the Pacific, twelve miles down Highway One from Carmel. Sims had never eaten at Rocky Point, too rich for a sheriff's salary.

"Last time you had that strange feeling, it turned out to be murder," Zip said as he opened the driver's door.

"Yeah," Tanner said, sliding into the passenger seat. His stomach growled. He'd missed breakfast, the whole damned day gone wrong, all because of this guy the Coast Guard had just hoisted from a cove at Rocky Point.

The call had come in at seven-forty that morning. A half-hour later Tanner and Zip stood on a barren outcropping over the ocean, a hundred yards south of the restaurant.

No fog, the last three days cloudless and warm, temperatures in the seventies, evenings almost balmy, the late Indian summer not too unusual for October. A sliver of sun inched over the undulating mountaintops, promising another hot day. Tanner unzipped his jacket and breathed air laden with traces of salt, seaweed, and dead fish. He hoped the Coast Guard got its ass down here soon. The Sheriff's Rescue Unit had been alerted but would take too long to assemble a team. Tanner glimpsed at his surroundings.

The restaurant huddled in a grove of cypress and Monterey pine twisted and stunted by constant winds. Cliffs to the north plunged into snarling waves and craggy rocks. In the distance to the south rose the parapet of Hurricane Point, the sweep of Big Sur's spectacular headlands defined by the sea's sharp blue horizon. Near where the officers stood was a generous open pasture sloping to the cliffs. A scattering of cattle grazed the brown grass. Tanner wondered if the cows had seen the victim sail over the cliff. He needed a witness.

"God almighty, how'd he get there?" Zip said, his binoculars fixed on the body in the cove directly below them.

"Now how the hell would I know?" Tanner shook his head; sometimes he was flat sure Zip had his feathers glued on wrong, acted kind of dumb. Other times, the boy – red-haired, good looking, and fast with the ladies – showed smarts. And Tanner had to admit he had probably been dumber at twenty-five, and never good looking or fast with the ladies.

He ran a hand over his thinning scalp. "First let's get the poor bastard out of there."

A small group of restaurant workers gathered around them. Tanner was glad there were no customers yet, didn't want a crowd. Lunch would be the first meal served, two hours away. His belly complained. He'd missed his bacon and eggs, biscuits. Black coffee wasn't enough to thwart hunger and a sour mood.

A young woman said, "Is he alive?"

Jesus H. Christ. Tanner threw an exasperated look over his shoulder, "Now if I knew that, I'd be a genius, right?"

He felt the little clutch of people press closer. Without looking at them, he said, "So how about not crowding me, huh? Next thing I'll be over the cliff myself." Tanner hated heights, something he'd never admit. The restaurant itself hung in what he considered an unnatural position, probably slide down the precipice into the Pacific some day.

"Gimme the binocs," he said. Zip pulled the strap over his head and gave the glasses to Tanner.

Tanner focused, shifting his magnified scan up to the meadow, then down the jagged granite cliff to where a body lay sprawled on the rocks. The man had on Levis, brown parka over gray shirt or sweater, tennis shoes. Waves exploded angry-white, spraying the victim. Farther out, there was no froth. Instead, giant blue swells rolled toward the bluffs; broken sunlight flashed aquamarine from their depths.

The glasses brought it too close for Tanner; he felt something akin to seasickness wash over him, like the stomach flu. The ocean's brackish odors didn't help.

"Jesus," he said, his brow all at once cold and wet. He handed the binoculars to Hessler. "Now I remember why I never joined the frigging Navy."

Just then a heavy thumping sound filled the air, like the slow beat of a dozen bass drums. The small gathering looked north to see a Coast Guard helicopter soar over the hump of the ridge, then slide offshore to follow the line of the cliff. It reminded Tanner of a giant, red-orange dragonfly.

Tanner keyed his portable radio, "Coast Guard, Sheriff Tanner Sims. Over."

Tanner and Zip watched the ambulance until it disappeared around a curve on the driveway leading to Highway One. They went into the restaurant and sat by a front window where Tanner sipped lukewarm coffee; the fragrance of fresh bread and seared beef stirred his digestive juices. He stared past the rocks to the far-off boundary of pale sky and dark water.

The panorama filled him with a sudden sense of being small and unneeded, like a random clump of kelp floating on that ocean. He wished away the shattered remains of the unknown DOA in the ambulance, the broken pieces of his job – every day more of the same. No surprise that he and Beth were drifting apart, the romance becoming a vague memory. So much crap. Every day more crap.

"You wanted to talk to me again?" the heavy German accent jolting Sims out of his reverie. A tall, angular man in his thirties with a handsome, serious face sat down.

"Yeah," Tanner said. "Holtz, isn't it?"

The Rocky Point manager nodded.

"You say you're here at seven-fifteen. Always that early?"

"No, today I'm expecting a special meat delivery." Holtz looked at his watch. "Schmuck's still not here."

"So, Holtz, when did you see the victim?"

"About seven-thirty, I walked out to the point to have a smoke. Saw the guy on the rocks and ran back to call 911."

"No one else around? On the cliff? Anywhere?"

"One man in the kitchen, baking. That's all."

"And you're sure no one here ever saw the deceased before?"

"That's what they say," Holtz said.

Tanner had insisted that the restaurant staff go through the grisly task of viewing the remains. One waitress came close to fainting at seeing the victim's head cracked open, every bone probably smashed. Male Caucasian, old fellow, looked close to eighty, sparse gray hair, needed a shave, reeked of booze. No I.D., his pockets held a handkerchief, twelve dollars and eighteen cents, and four tiny blue pills which no one could identify. The pills had sent a warning buzz up and down Tanner's spine, like when he had to enter a suspicious house looking for God knows what. His forehead tightened.

"Coroner says no evidence of other causes of death, not yet anyway." He looked at Zip. "So why no I.D.?"

The deputy shrugged.

Shit. Tanner stood, the others followed suit. He and Zip walked out the front entrance and to the car.

As Zip aimed the Ford up the rise toward the highway, it came to Tanner, like seeing a crime investigation on TV.

"Stop!"

The deputy slammed on the brake, pitching them both against the seat belts. "Jesus, Tanner! What is it?"

"Go back to the lot. We got to take a hike."

After parking, they thrashed through brown grass, scrub oak and chaparral until they got to the site outlined with yellow tape, where the Coast Guard crew had hoisted up the DOA into the helicopter. A quarter mile away Tanner could see the lunch customers' cars pulling into the restaurant. He got a gnawing urge for some of Rocky Point's famous prime rib.

"Whew! Thought we were done with all this walking," Zip said, gulping air. "Glad the poison oak ain't in full growth."

"Yeah, well, like I said, I need another look." Tanner stepped over the tape and edged his way to the brink of the cliff. The grass had been heavily matted by officers and rescuers. Ten feet from the edge Tanner went down on all fours and crawled to the edge to do a quick survey of the rocks and seething tide. He retreated and got to his feet.

On the other side of the crime scene tape he came on a trace of mashed grass separate from the other. He followed the ill-defined trail for a few yards until it dissolved in brush and rocky ground.

"Let's find this trail if we can," Tanner said. "Stay out of the cow piles." Heads down, the officers walked in tandem, several feet apart.

"Here!" Zip said, pointing at some more flattened grass.

Tanner joined him. They continued and came to a bare piece of ground, the dust marked by footprints, two distinct sets, one larger than the other.

"Goddamnit. I knew it." He hadn't known it, but what the hell, take credit where you can. Impresses young deputies.

Another seventy-five yards brought them to a barbed wire fence. On the other side of it was Highway One, the promise of a hundred more miles of breathtaking coast road to Morro Bay.

They wormed through the wire. To find footprints was impossible; the wide highway pull-off was a red-dusted jumble of tire tracks and cigarette butts. Nothing to hang your hat on.

"Bring the car up here, Zip."

"Geez, Sheriff, got to be a mile back there to the car."

"Well, no shit, James Bond! Go get the car! I'll be down there with those prints. Bring me the plaster kit."

Sims drank coffee and argued on the phone. "I can't believe this. Tell her to take a flying leap!" He swung his chair around to stare at the County Building's parking lot, the thick pine forest behind it.

He said, "I'll call you back," and pounded the receiver into the cradle. Another fight with the Board of Supervisors, this time about the color of the new sheriffs' cars. Jesus.

The phone rang; Tanner picked up. "Sheriff Sims."

"Coroner's office, Tracy Flint."

"Hey, Tracy. Got anything?" He listened.

"Blood alcohol enough to put a man to sleep. No foul play, just plain-assed drunk. Impact on the rocks killed him."

"What about the pills?" Tanner said.

"You're gonna love this. We make the DOA to be late seventies. The pills are Viagra!"

Tanner guffawed and said, "So the poor bastard died happy!"

She giggled. "Or died trying. Want the pills?"

"Not unless you come with them," he said.

"You're a dirty old man, but I still love you."

"So does my wife. Stay away from me, sweet thing."

Tracy laughed and hung up.

Tanner kept the phone to his ear. For a fleeting moment he thought of calling Beth, sharing some of his day with her, but the idea passed. Instead, he punched an internal number and Zip came on the line.

"So here's what the coroner says." Tanner related his conversation with Tracy Flint.

Zip chuckled at the Viagra remarks.

Tanner said, "How'd the horny bastard get there? Walk? Too drunk to drive. Oh yeah, on the plaster casts – his are '98 Nike's, others are woman's Reebocks, no year."

"The woman had to drive him there, he was that shit-faced."

"You're getting good, Hessler. Make detective some day. So get a sketch done of him, check missing persons, mosey down the coast, ask around. Maybe someone knows the guy."

Zip said, "Will do," and signed off.

Tanner took a bamboo back-scratcher from his drawer to attack the phantom itch. He had a bizarre vision of old Farley, in the nude, sailing off the cliff with a raging hard-on.

Zip made it down to Big Sur in forty-five minutes. The rustic hamlet was tucked into groves of redwoods and spruce and encircled by tree-covered hillsides that kept the place in perpetual shade; even on this sunlit morning it felt cool. Big Sur consisted of a gas station, a handful of restaurants, a scattering of small retail shops and a few cabins. Most of the two hundred residents lived in steep canyons meandering to the east, their solitude guarded by rugged terrain and a mind-your-own-business approach to life.

Zip parked by the River Inn, a drinking and eating establishment frequented by locals. The frame building squatted on the banks of the shallow Big Sur River.

He entered and angled toward the cocktail lounge where a couple of men sat at a table talking in low tones. He took a stool at the bar. The girl behind the counter was in her thirties and pretty, right out of the Sixties, he thought – no makeup, straight auburn hair to the waist, levis, lots of earrings, a tiny heart tattooed on the top of her wrist.

"Hi, sheriff," she said, giving him a warm smile.

He grinned. "Deputy, actually."

"Good enough for me. What can I get you?"

"How about coffee?"

She swung around and went to a nearby hot plate, poured from the pot, placed the mug in front of Zip.

"Thanks," he said and put a five on the bar.

"First one's on me," she said, sliding the money at him. "I'm Dana Richards." She extended her hand.

He took it. "Zip Hessler," he said, aware he was blushing.

"Sightseeing?" There was a hint of sarcasm.

"Couldn't be any prettier scenery around here than you." He knew it was a tacky line but she smiled. Classy dame, Zip thought. "Sure appreciate it if you could help me out." He slipped the sketch from his jacket pocket and laid it on the polished surface.

"Ever see this guy?"

Dana examined the image. The police artist had drawn a picture of a wrinkled man with sparse gray hair and eyes the same color, lips stretched thin, unsmiling. An angry scar ran from under one eye to the corner of his mouth.

She frowned. "Farley Sears. Lives up Dry Creek Canyon," caution in her reply. "What about him?"

"Found him on the cliffs Thursday."

"Dead?"

"Dead," Zip said.

Dana's face turned ashen. "God. Poor Flo."

Zip guided the Dodge sedan over the ruts, certain he'd bust the oil pan any minute. The unpaved road, now narrowed to a car width, meandered four miles from Highway One, struggling up through a sunless, forested canyon. No place to turn around other than occasional entrances to unseen cabins.

He hated doing this. First time he'd ever had to notify a next of kin, not sure how he'd handle it.

The directions Dana Richards had given him held true. He intended to drop back by and thank her, see if maybe she'd go out with him. Around the next hairpin turn was a ramshackle gate, a concoction of boards lashed together by baling wire. He got out, opened the gate and drove through a grove of redwoods, then stopped to scrutinize the cabin lurking in the forest – pine logs, rusted metal roof, TV dish attached. A dented Chevy pickup with a camper shell sat in front. He climbed onto the tiny porch, rapped at the wooden door and waited.

Thirty seconds later the door creaked open, a woman peered out. She looked even older than Farley, a hollow face, pinched mouth, her stooped, thin body shrunk into the flowered dress like she was hiding in it, the hem drooping over black, ankle-top boots. Not Reebocks.

"Mrs. Sears?"

"Yeah?" Quiet, suspicious.

"I'm Deputy Sheriff Hessler. About your husband, ma'am."

"He ain't here. Ain't seen him for three days." She paused, her eyes narrowed, as if she were examining a wall calendar in her mind. "Yeah, been three days."

"May I come in?" Zip felt awkward, self-conscious. How did he tell a woman her husband had crushed his body in a rocky cove, that he wouldn't be home?

She hesitated, then opened the door wider and he entered, looked around. Three, maybe four rooms, kitchen to the left of the front room. Rear windows showed a littered yard overrun by weeds, plus a neat row of mature cannabis plants. He made a note of it, come back later and chop it down.

"You looking at Mary Jane out yonder?" she said. "She's legal, sheriff. I got the Big C, lungs about gone, fifty years smoking. Camels and Luckies. Mary Jane helps me take my medicine, holds my food down."

"It's okay, ma'am." He showed her the sketch.

"That's Farley. He in some kind of trouble?" she said.

"We found him in a cove at Rocky Point." He paused, having trouble with what he had to say. "Hate to have to tell you this.

He's gone, ma'am. Fall killed him."

Her somber face registered nothing; he'd even say she was apathetic. Florence Sears looked off, her dull gray eyes focused beyond the windows, beyond the wall of trees, as if there was something out there Zip couldn't see.

"He drinking?"

"Looks that way, ma'am."

"Always drank too much," as if she were castigating Farley himself.

"Mrs. Sears, this may be painful for you, but I'll have to ask you to follow me into Monterey to identify the body."

Fifteen minutes later Zip wheeled north onto Highway One with Flo Sears – not exactly acting like what he'd call a devastated widow – trailing him in her old pickup. He radioed Tanner they were on the way.

"Okay," Tanner said, "I'll get a warrant and hightail it down there, check out the Sears' place."

Sims noticed the marijuana in the yard, shook his head. Not worth chasing – probably his kids had kept bigger stashes. He snapped on rubber gloves and tested the rear door. Unlocked.

A cluttered kitchen, last week's dishes in the sink. A few worn pieces of furniture in the living room, fifteen-inch TV. Family pictures on the walls, several on the mantle over the tiny fireplace, including a photo of a Navy chief petty officer and a pretty girl in a suit, corsage pinned to her lapel. Farley and Flo, Tanner guessed. He went to the rumpled bedroom, opened drawers, looked in the closet, then checked the bathroom.

The medicine cabinet held bottles of prescriptions for her. Stuff he'd never heard of, prescribed by a Monterey oncologist. Looked like the lady had serious problems. Farley's only pills were from the VA Clinic pharmacy, for blood pressure.

Tanner returned to the kitchen. He rummaged through the trashcan – banana peels, milk cartons, beer bottles, papers, coffee grounds, rotted lettuce. Wadded up in a Scott towel was an empty brown medicine vial, prescribed by a Salinas physician: Viagra, use as directed. The phantom itch struck again. He wrapped the container in his handkerchief and went out the door. A lean-to work shed was at the rear of the property. He gave it a quick going-over. Rusted saws, shovels, garden tools, pots. A pair of dirt caked shoes on a shelf. Reebocks. Good for tilling marijuana and walks with your husband. He went to the car and got the plaster kit.

The next morning Tanner called Zip into his office and said, "How'd Mrs. Sears take it?"

Zip said, "Real cool at the house, like she didn't give a damn. That way right up until she looked under the sheet in the morgue. Then she kind of fell apart, cried pretty hard. Had to sit down and have a glass of water."

"All the parts don't fit," Tanner said.

Zip gave him a quizzical look.

"Cast of her shoes checks out with the ones in the field. Trying to get hold of the doctor in Salinas." Tanner frowned. "What the hell was Viagra doing in his pockets?"

"Kind of crazy," Zip said.

"Let's take a drive down, visit the grieving widow."

The pickup was parked on the far side of the house. Zip eased the car alongside and the two officers got out. Tanner went ahead. Zip stayed a few paces behind, and halted at the end of the house, just in case. Florence Sears was bent over a marijuana plant, short hoe in hand.

She straightened and swung around to greet the men with narrowed eyes, her knuckles white on the handle.

"Ma'am," Tanner said.

"Sheriff," she said, dropping the hoe at her feet, by a mud-encrusted Reebock.

"Wonder if we could have a word?" She's just plain worn

out, Tanner thought. God, all she's got left is a patch of cannabis ready for harvest, and Death lying on her shoulder. He had an urge to walk away, leave it be. Who gives a shit?

"Mrs. Sears, before you say anything..." He stated her rights, then started the small tape recorder.

She took a deep breath. "Doesn't matter. Last Wednesday. I found those blue pills, told him. He said he was saving them for a special time with me. Goddamn lie. No sex for us in six or seven years, since I got sick. He was banging some bitch up Palo Colorado Canyon. Count on it, I know. It gets around."

"Ma'am, you don't have to..." Tanner began.

She cut him off. "He was drunk, like every night. I say to him, okay, you swallow down a couple of those little blue jewels and let's go to Rocky Point, to the field – our field. Wednesday night was warm, just like before."

Zip walked up and stood next to the sheriff. Tanner gave the deputy a quick glance.

"Like before? Tanner said.

"Rocky Point... the first place we made love after we moved here, just out of the Navy. Sounds kind of dumb now, I guess." She stopped, as if expecting Tanner to say something.

He blushed, couldn't think of a reply, halfway convinced that this was another woman, another time.

Her voice drifted lower, becoming husky and sensuous. "We were full of cheap wine and came out to Rocky Point. We didn't even know that was the name of the place, we came out to see the sunset. It was a rich, sexy night, full of stars, a piece of moon, hot wind from the mountains." She lifted her head to stare at the sea mist pouring in overhead, at the shadowed crowns of redwoods and firs, her eyes mirroring a faraway place. "It was wild, steamy love. Delicious, exciting love."   A short silence. "Real love."

Tanner saw the semblance of a smile form. His gut knotted up. God, he thought, she's a poet. Under that tough hide she's all poetry. She tosses beautiful, pure lyrics to the wind, not even aware of them. Kind of the way he scratched dumb little poems on scraps of paper, wadding them up and tossing them in the wastebasket. He used to share them with Beth. No more.

"We walked down through the field, down to the cliff, and we stood there." Her eyes glistened. "In the warm wind."

Tanner said, "This was when you got out of the Navy?"

She gave him a look as if he were an idiot. "I mean last Wednesday night." She went back to watching the sky. "The cliff," she said. A long pause. "Such warm wind...."

"Yes, ma'am, the cliff," Tanner said, attempting to keep her, and himself, on track.

"Farley..." she wavered, keeping her eyes on the heavens. "Farley spoke mean. He says 'What the hell's got into you? What the hell we standing around here for?'"

She stopped, then in a flat, matter-of-fact tone, Flo said, "I pushed him off."

Hair prickled on Tanner's neck, his hand tightened on the recorder. He said, "You mean you...?"

"Don't you see?" Tears welled up.

Tanner felt embarrassment rush through him like he remembered when he saw his mother cry for the first time. He wanted to reach her, he didn't know how.

Now her words flowed soft and cool and gray like the fog. "Sheriff, I could feel him looking at me, out there in the dark, dropping off that cliff. And I knew what he was saying..." She hesitated. "He was saying, 'Why, Flo? Why?'"

Maybe ten seconds passed, then she looked straight at Tanner, her red eyes filled with conviction.

"And I said because you forgot, Farley. You forgot."

Another Kind of View

BY MARY CLARKSON

Another Kind of View
BY MARY CLARKSON

The sunset over the Pacific had been breathtaking, brilliant, with no hint of worsening weather such as the local forecaster predicted.

At Rocky Point Restaurant, the earliest diners who had driven fifteen miles down from the Monterey resort area to enjoy the sunset from the dining room were well rewarded. Now the flames in the sky were fading, streaking to a gloomy gray over the ocean, but the drama of the spotlighted cliffs and rocks still diverted the attention of the diners from their after dinner coffee and conversation.

Wait staff moved a little more slowly now, refilling cups, totaling checks, collecting credit cards. Soon enough the eight o'clock crowd would ease out of the bar and head for the vacating tables. Then the hurry-up, in and out of the kitchen would resume. Some of the guests were already strolling through the long, narrow northern part of the restaurant toward a private room in the back.

At a table in the main dining room, a well-tailored, lean and graying, middle-aged man in city clothes leaned toward his much younger dinner partner, nodding toward one of them.

"Clint Eastwood," he murmured.

His date turned around, recognized the star, and started to reach for her purse, for a pen, for a menu, anything. But the moment passed. Eastwood glanced down, smiled, and continued on, following his wife, Dina. They vanished into the private dining room, trailed by several other well-dressed couples.

"Amy will shoot me," she said to her companion..."Clint was that close and I didn't get his autograph. Didn't even get a good look at him."

"Probably just as well," he replied. "This is his home territory. He deserves to be left alone."

Back in the private room, several groups were already seated, enjoying drinks and beginning conversations. Horst, the maitre d' and Dieter, a waiter who had been at the restaurant for some thirty years, moved briskly to set up extra places. At a table set aside from the others, the party was just gathering and being greeted by their hostess, who then moved on to meet the newest arrivals.

In the main dining area, the appearance of the Eastwoods, as well as other recognizable couples on their way to the private room had distracted the rest of the guests. Aside from one retired Navy Captain who was well into his favorite war story and knew of no reason to stop until it ran its well-spun course, all attention was focused on the passage of the "celebrities." But, once they disappeared, things returned to normal. Conversations resumed, punctuated by the clink of glassware and china.

The city man turned to his pretty partner once more.

"Now, what do you think? Wasn't that sky worth the drive down?"

She paused, her mind still on the missed opportunity for an autograph. "Oh yes. This is a wonderful place."

He smiled at her.

It was really incredible how much she looked like his daughter. The dark brown eyes and hair curling slightly, even the dimple showing in her cheek as she looked around the room, determined not to miss another famous person. How young she looked, even though she'd sworn to him she was 21!

"How about dessert?" he offered.

"Oh no, I really couldn't."

"They have a wonderful selection here. Surely you're not worried about your weight?"

My God, the girl was actually blushing! And she was really very slender.

She ventured, "Shouldn't we be getting back to San Francisco?"

"All in good time. At least have some coffee. I plan to, and a brandy as well."

Resigned, she sighed, "If you think we really have time." Then excused herself to visit the ladies room.

Left alone, he felt himself slipping into a dark cloud of nostalgia.

He well remembered the last time he was here. His daughter was with him then. They'd had a wonderful dinner. Since his wife deserted, he usually served wine at home to the two of them, even though Julie was technically under drinking age. But here, in the restaurant that night she had taken a few too many sips from his wine glass. That's when she began teasing him about her future plans.

He roused himself from the memory when his companion returned.

"I'm sorry," she apologized. "There were others ahead of me".

He nodded, forcing a smile. "Isn't that always the way! Now, how about that brandy?"

He gestured to Dieter, who hovered in the background, and placed an order for two.

"When we're finished here, there's something I would like to show you, another kind of view."

She was startled. "Really? It's getting pretty dark."

He shrugged. "The stars will be out. And there's light from the restaurant. Besides, I could use some fresh air before we start driving back."

He watched with some amusement as she took a tentative sip of the brandy and tried to disguise a shudder.

He sensed her embarrassment. She was probably used to beer - that was the drink of choice for a college budget. But she seemed more enthusiastic with the second sip, and lifted her glass again.

It wouldn't be long now. He looked at the other diners, feeling some urgency. But they were all engrossed in their own conversations. He tried to relax. At least no one had seemed interested in their table by the window.

He looked back at her again, knowing he had to mask the turmoil inside. " I heard of something today that might interest you. About a new company forming. They'll be hiring staff. I could arrange an interview if you like."

She looked up, eager. "That would be so kind. I still haven't found anything that pays enough, with rents so high." She flushed. "I was almost thinking I'd have to go back home after all."

There it was again. Her expression, so like Julie. Wistful, and yet - so determined. And yes, the memories were back. They made it hard to breathe.

He signaled for the check.

As they left the shelter of the main entrance, she shivered. It was colder and the wind was up. He took her arm in a firm grip, guiding her to the left, to the rear of the main building, away from the parking lot. She stumbled. It was difficult to see.

"Should have remembered my flashlight," he mumbled. But his feet soon found the too familiar path. They passed behind a darkened cabin, past the dumpster, rusting refuse cans, a pile of lumber.

Through a grove of cypress, sculpted by the wind, the ocean glimmered in the moonlight beyond the rocks below. He led her forward down the slope, then paused. She was trembling.

The memory was back resurrecting the pain. Julie was here, after all. She had never left. She was teasing him . She thought she was in love.

Of course she couldn't be. She was still a little girl. And of course she couldn't leave him, that's what her mother did. Julie belonged to him. He would keep his little girl with him, always.

"Just a little further now. The path is safe."

"Please. It's so cold. Can't we go back now?"

"There's something I want to share with you - we can't quite see from here."

They were close to the rocks now, standing on wet grass near the cliff edge above, looking out to sea. It wasn't far down to the jagged rocks and crashing surf. Looked like the tide was in.

And the memory was back.

"Listen to me, Julie!"

She gazed at him, trying to understand. "My name isn't Julie, you know that."

"Julie, I don't want to lose you again. You mustn't leave me now!"

Sudden fear clutched at her throat and weakened her knees. She pulled away and began to scramble up the path. But as she slipped and almost fell on the slippery grass, he grabbed her arm and held her up.

"Julie. You mustn't run away. Not this time!"

The stiffening breeze rustled through the shadowed underbrush. The surf's roar merged with the echo of his own excited breathing. He hardly heard her pleading.

"Please, I need to go back. I promised I'd be back in town early tonight. You told me we would."

"Julie, I told you to forget that boy. There's no room in your life for him now. We have plans, you and I. We have to think of our future..."

It grew darker as the moon drifted behind a cloudbank. He yanked at her arm, and as she lost balance, threw his other arm around her shoulders and pushed her back down the slope. She slipped again, and still again, as he urged her toward the cliff edge.

Her voice turned shrill, " Please, I'm so cold. Let's go back to the car."

It was then that he felt the first drops of rain on his face.

That made it perfect. Just like the first time. The storm was sure to follow.

As if answering his thoughts, thunder echoed in the distance. And as the rain grew heavy, a flash of lightning revealed her terrified face. With a violent effort she broke away, twisting, then tumbling over the cliff's edge, and down. Down, missing the rocks, into the churning sea.

He shook his head and closed his eyes.

Julie would never learn. But she wouldn't leave him now.

Several months later, Dieter was filling in for Darlene at the front desk while she took a break. When the door opened, he smiled his professional welcome at the couple who were entering.

The man was lean, middle-aged, well tailored, graying, carefully groomed. The young woman with him, (young enough to be his daughter), was very slender, with dark brown eyes and hair just slightly curling, a dimple showing in her cheek as she looked toward the dining room.

Horst appeared, menus in hand, and led them to a table by the window. Once settled, the man leaned forward, "Now, what do you think about that view? Isn't it worth the drive down?"

She glanced at him before her gaze wandered to inspect the room. "This is a wonderful place."

He smiled at her.

It was amazing how much she looked like Julie, even to the dimple in her cheek. How young she looked!

He scanned his menu quickly. "I would recommend any of the fish dishes. They're known for fish."

She nodded, replacing her menu on the tabletop. "I'll just have what you're having."

"Very well," he approved, signaled to Dieter and gave the order. As Dieter hurried away, he said, "There, my dear. Now, we can concentrate on the sunset."

She nodded. "The sky is beautiful."

"There will be lights on the rocks soon. And, when we're finished here, after our brandy, there's something I've been wanting to show you, it's very...special. Another kind of view."

What are the Odds?

BY LAURA PASTEN

What are the Odds?
BY LAURA PASTEN

The policewoman pointed to pictures of women's hairdos. "Normally, in the majority of rape cases hair style and length play a key role. Rapists almost always pick women with long hair, a pony tail or braid, a means to grab and control their victims."

Robin looked at her best friend's long, black curly hair and frowned. She looked around at the other Neighborhood Watch Reps, grateful to see that her hair was the shortest.

"You might think that most rapes occur at night, but statistics show that the majority of rapes occur between five and eight o'clock in the morning, often in parking lots. But none of the sixteen rapes in Monterey County during the last six months fit this profile."

Beth's eyebrows arched in surprise. She leaned toward Robin, "Did you know there were sixteen? I didn't see anything in the papers, did you?"

Robin shook her head as she changed cassettes in her tape recorder.

The profiler continued. "That's because these latest rapes don't involve women being over-powered physically; these rape victims are being compromised chemically. And the chemical is Rohypnolóa: colorless, odorless, tasteless chemical placed in the victims' beverage which makes them walking zombies that the rapist can lead away to his chosen rape site, leaving them with total amnesia or the inability to describe their assailant."

Beth whispered, "You ever heard of that stuff?"

Robin nodded. "Yeah, we use it at the hospital – some of the doctors use it for minor surgical procedures. I heard they busted some guys over at the Defense Language Institute for making the stuff in a lab. It's readily available. Great, huh?"

"...and like I said, we have DNA tested sperm from these latest victims, but it doesn't match anyone presently in our files." The policewoman noticed a number of people were fidgeting and looking at their watches. "Okay, let's all take a lunch break. Be back in one hour."

Amid the scraping of chairs and people rustling lunch sacks, Robin carefully layered a dill pickle in between two pieces of jack cheese. Beth watched with a pained look on her face as Robin gazed at her favorite sandwich for a few seconds before gulping it down, all except for a bite for each of the geese, of course. When she was done, she eyed Beth's lunch. "Save something for Frankie and Annie."

"I know, I know. When haven't I?" Beth said, grinning. "Let's go out and see those long-necked varmints now, so I can give them these pieces of apple."

As they neared Robin's Bronco, they saw Frankie and Annie snaking their long necks out the opened window calling to them. "Erhonk, erhonk!" People were already starting to congregate around the vehicle; the two geese never failed to gain an audience.

As usual, Robin had them in harnesses with diapers. Frankie sported a bow tie at the base of his neck, and Annie had a little flowered skirt tucked under her wings.

Robin had started them out with harnesses and diapers and little outfits from the time they were one day old, so they had never known anything different. Since they were raised in the house, even slept in Robin and Sal's bed snuggled up to Robin's backside, they acted more like people than birds. Intelligent, loving and highly motivated by food, they learned new tricks daily. Robin doted on them and took them everywhere.

She opened the car door and leaned over. "Okay, give mama a hug." They took turns stretching their long necks over her shoulder and snuggling up to Robin. She attached leashes to their harnesses.

"Okay, let's go potty." They jumped into her arms, and she carefully set them down, undoing their diapers and leading them to a patch of grass. Frankie and Annie promptly did their business. "Good kids," Robin cooed. At the sound of the praise, they both pranced and danced in circles. "Erhonk, erhonk."

A man with a camera squatted down to take their picture. The geese rushed him with loud honking and angry hisses, forcing the man into a hasty retreat.

"Best guard geese in the country," Robin declared. She looked toward Beth. "Today I discovered they like roses. Sal sent me flowers last night. This morning there's only a few tattered stems."

Beth laughed. "That husband of yours is too good to be true. Flowers, huh? You ever worry about him being unfaithful, since he's out of town so much?"

"No way. We were watching a TV program about infidelity last year, and he kissed me and said, 'Why would I eat hamburger when I can eat filet mignon?' I wish he were home more, but not for that reason."

Beth pretended to stick her finger down her throat and gag. They both laughed. "Seriously, though," Beth said, "I do worry about you being alone so much, what with that crazed rapist-killer we have loose on the peninsula. Be careful!"

"I will, and, besides, I have short hair, nothing to grab," she said, running her fingers through her blond curls. "And Frankie and Annie will protect me. Right, kids? Show them your karate moves." Both geese promptly jumped with one foot extended straight out. The people around them howled, demanding more.

Beth shook her head. "Amazing your patients don't mind having a demented doctor who carts two geese around with her, and who always wears the same damn sweatshirt."

Robin pretended to be hurt as she looked down at her sweatshirt with the words "Remember, Raccoons Are Your Friends" across the front. "Frankie and Annie, tell the rude lady what you think of her." She gave a hand signal, and the geese promptly hissed in unison. Everyone laughed, then groaned their disappointment as she put them back into the car.

Beth sipped her Chardonnay as she looked out the window at the ever-changing scene of the waves crashing against the rocks at Rocky Point Restaurant.

"I'm back," Robin said, as she sat down.

Beth pushed a mass of black curls back over her ear. "So where were you?"

"Where else – the bathroom. Ever since Weight Watchers and their 'drink 8 glasses a day', that's all I ever do, it seems," Robin said. She glanced down and noticed a spot on her sweatshirt. She dipped her napkin into her water glass and dabbed furiously at the offending stain.

"Your cell phone rang; call ID said it was your husband. I looked in the bathroom. No one was there," Beth said.

"Let me guess. You looked under the stall doors for feet, right?"

"Yeah, why?"

"Well, you know how in the movies, the killers always look under the stall doors for feet, and when they see them, they shoot through the doors and kill the poor sap inside? When I'm in a public restroom, I always get nervous. For some reason I always pick up my feet so no one can see them, a quirky habit."

Beth laughed. "That's one of the reasons I like you. You're weird! By the way, I heard a joke that's right up your alley. What's the difference between kinky and perverted?"

Robin shrugged.

"Kinky is when you use a feather, and perverted is when you use the whole chicken."

Robin groaned and rolled her eyes. "Talk about a weirdo, look in the mirror." She got her cell phone out of her backpack and called Sal back.

"Hi, Hon," Robin said, then listened. "No, I'm still not up to par. Beth met me here at Rocky Point to cheer me up. You know they have that marvelous garlic cheese bread." She listened. "Babe, I told you. Antibiotics only work for bacteria, and I have the flu, a virus. Trust me!" She tapped her foot while he talked. "Okay, see you this weekend. Hopefully, I'll feel better by then." She hung up with a sigh.

"He wants you to take antibiotics?" Beth said.

"Yeah, he's on this business trip in Chicago, be back in two days. He calls every day, asks if I'm over this darn flu, then insists that I take antibiotics because he's worried about me. Geez, as a doctor I ought to know if I should take antibiotics or not. Men!" She continued dabbing at her sweatshirt.

Beth grimaced. "Maybe now you'll wear something else. How many of those do you have anyway? Or do you just keep wearing the same one over and over?"

Robin acted hurt. "I love this sweatshirt. Matter of fact, I bought one for you, too." She handed a package to Beth.

Beth rolled her eyes. "Thanks, I guess. Next, you'll probably give me a pair of geese so I can act just as goofy as you."

Just then the waiter arrived with a cooled bottle of Dom Perignon. "A gentleman named Sal, your husband, I believe, called and ordered this to be delivered to you."

Robin smiled. "Like I said, he's one in a million."

The man stroked his mustache as he eyed the two coeds at a nearby table, trying to catch their eye so he could flash them his famous smile. Deep in conversation, they failed to be captivated, so he returned his attention to his friend, Dick, a beefy no-neck man with a beer belly who sat across from him. Dick's face had a sort of robust look to it, but his cheeks were red from dozens of broken little veins. He downed his fifth beer and tilted his head to signal the bartender for another.

The blond, mustached guy sat tall, puffing out his chest and positioning his iron-pumped arms to advantage. He ran his fingers through his hair, making sure that a "devil may care" lock spilled down his forehead, then peered sideways towards the girls' table to see if they had noticed. He fidgeted and tapped his fingers on the table, thinking that the little redhead sure was something. He abruptly stood, catching his chair before it could topple over.

"Dick, I'll be right back. Something I have to do." He strutted past the table with the two coeds, glancing over his shoulder to see if he had their attention. He scowled. They didn't appear to notice him.

He strode into the men's room, glanced around, then took a pinch of powder from a vial in his jacket pocket. His lips curled into a smile as he tilted his head in acknowledgment of his handsome image in the mirror, his fingertips still holding their sinister cargo. His heartbeat quickened, and his forehead glistened in anticipation as he walked back through the bar. He paused to study the girl; his tongue flicked in and out. The pixie redhead, yeah, that's the one.

As he neared the table, he heard parts of the conversation, "...exam....got to get an A...."

He leaned over. "Scuse me, ladies, do you know that guy over there?" Their heads turned in the direction he was pointing, toward a black man who seemed startled by their attention. He dropped the powder into his victim's glass. Both girls turned back toward him. The redhead said, "No, why?"

He leaned in and lowered his voice. "That man hasn't taken his eyes off of you since you got here. He looks like trouble. Thought I should warn you...just be careful."

The girls thanked him, then glared at the hapless black fellow.

He stroked his mustache as he sauntered back to his table and sat down.

Dick furrowed his brow. "So what the hell was that all about? What's up with that guy?"

He shrugged. "Nothin', had to get them to look away, that's all. I merely suggested he was leering at them."

"You're using that date rape shit again, aren't you?"

He tapped his breast pocket. "It's called Rohypnol, man. Makes 'em nauseous, malleable AND they black out, don't remember a fuckin' thing. It's positively beautiful."

"Makes 'em want to puke? And that's good?"

"Yeah, makes them go to the restroom, and guess who's there to lead them to temptation, give them a special treat."

Dick pushed away from the table. "You sick fuck. I don't want any part of this rape shit."

He clamped an iron grip on Dick's arm. "You sure? Man, the stuff is amazing; you can lead them away like babies, do it in the car, alley. They don't care or remember. Sweet nooky, as much as you want."

Dick shook his head in disgust. "You got that sweet, gorgeous wife. Why you fuckin' around like this? Christ, if she were mine...."

The blonde man slammed his beer mug down on the table.

"That's it. I've thought of the perfect bet for our poker game tonight." He gazed off into space as he pondered the details. "What are the odds? How about if I lose, you can fuck that gorgeous, sweet, wife of mine; and if you lose, you pay up $5,000? Sound fair enough? Got to go, man. Catch you later." He strode toward the bathroom.

Dick hesitated, then sat back down as the redhead walked unsteadily toward the restroom. He watched Sal walk up, glance furtively toward her friend to make sure she wasn't watching, then wrapped his arm around her shoulder, guiding her out the side door.

Dick shook his head. "No way, man." He stared down at his beer for a few moments. "Oh, what the hell," he muttered then got up to follow.

Robin turned up the volume on her tape recorder. The angry sounds of the torrential rain and occasional thunder outside made it difficult to hear. She was replaying the tape she had made from the policewoman's talk about the rapes in Monterey County. She shuddered when she heard the recounting of how three of the rape victims had their throats slit from ear to ear. She grabbed her throat protectively, shivering from a gust of wind. What was that noise? She glanced at the open door, then her watch. It had been ten minutes since she let Frankie and Annie out to potty. Why hadn't they returned?

She walked out onto the porch, calling into the night, "Frankie! Annie!" She peered into the shadows of her front yard, squinting to see in the darkness. Two houses down, a car started up and drove off. What if they'd been hit by a car, their inert little bodies lying in the rain? She felt icy fingers of fear gnawing up her spine. With her most authoritative tone, she called, "Frankie! Annie! Come now!" No responding "erhonk, erhonk." No sound of web feet plopping through the mud, no sight of her long-necked winged angels.

A lump formed in her throat, making it difficult to swallow or breathe. "Oh, God, please don't let anything happen to them." She sprinted inside, grabbed a flashlight and dashed outside, not bothering to grab a coat.

Hours later, Robin dragged home, sneakers sloshing, tears and raindrops coursing down her cheeks. She trudged in, collapsing in a chair, unaware of her muddy footprints or the water pooling on the cushions. Frankie and Annie had vanished. Her unblinking eyes focused straight ahead on an image of little Annie when she had just hatched, a piece of eggshell on her head like a funny hat. Her mind jumped to the time in the garden when a coiled rattler was about to strike, and Frankie came from out of nowhere, attacked the snake, driving it off to save her, and in the process getting bitten. She had nursed him night and day for over a week, unsure whether he would live. Yes, they were buddies, counted on each other. But now, she had failed them, allowed them to come into harm's way.

Robin started trembling, then shaking uncontrollably. She needed to call and talk to Sal; he'd know what to do. Her hands shook so hard that it wasn't until the third try that she managed to push the correct numbers for the hotel in Chicago.

"Chicago Hilton," the receptionist answered.

"May I speak to Sal Kaufman, please? He's staying there."

There was a pause. "Mr. Kaufman checked out yesterday. Sorry."

Robin turned the phone off, hugged herself and rocked back and forth. "Damn, now I don't know how to reach him. Damn, damn, damn." Long moments passed before she grabbed the phone and called Beth.

No one answered. Beth probably had the ring turned off for the night. She left a message on the answering machine: "Beth, Frankie and Annie have disappeared. I'm going to look for them again in the morning, but I have to go into work in the afternoon to do a surgery. I should be home around six o'clock. Could you meet me here? You know where the key is. Let yourself in if I'm late."

She walked to the open door again, called out in a sort of prayer, "Frankie, Annie. . .I love you. Please come home...."

Robin stretched her neck from side to side. That was one tough surgery she had just completed. She glanced at her watch. She was late as usual, but Beth, God bless her, would understand.

She heard the sirens long before she rounded the corner and saw the ambulance and police cars in front of her house. She tasted bile rising in her throat, and her hands started to shake. She stopped the car in the middle of the road, ran out without turning off the engine or closing the car door.

"What's wrong? What happened? This is my house!"

A policeman waved her through. "See Captain Townsend inside."

She sprinted toward the front door, then stopped as two ambulance attendants came out carrying a stretcher. What looked like a body was under a sheet. "Wait!" she said. She reached toward the sheet, paused, took a deep breath and inched it back. The first thing she saw was a mass of black curls. Oh, my God! Beth, it was Beth! Blood covered her neck and chest, blood all over her sweatshirt, the one she had just given Beth yesterday.

She felt light-headed and queasy, and staggered into the yard where she leaned over and vomited until there were just dry heaves. She half-fell, half-sat down in the grass, and watched as the ambulance drove away, siren blaring. She felt as if she were in a tunnel, looking at blurred images through the wrong end of a telescope.

The policeman, presumably the Captain, walked up to her. She stood as he said, "This your house? I'm Captain Townsend. Who was that poor lady? Looks like she was murdered, throat was cut."

"My best friend. Beth...Murdered?" She stared at the policeman.

"Looks like someone must have been waiting inside the house. No signs of forced entry. We have to wait for Forensics, but she could be another victim of the rapist. She related to you?"

Seeing her expression, his face and tone softened. "I'm sorry, but I have to ask you these questions now, seems like speed is everything for success in solving murder cases."

Robin's face went slack, her mouth open as if to speak, but no words came out. The Captain shifted weight uneasily. "Miss?"

"Friend. She is...was...." Her voice trailed off. "We were supposed to....I told her to let herself in..." she whispered.

He studied her. "Same sweatshirt."

She followed his eyes to her shirt. She nodded. "I just gave it to...wear mine all the time." She attempted a smile as she glanced down at her raccoon sweatshirt.

The policeman was deep in thought. "Possibly the killer thought she was you?"

The last thing she remembered was his look of concern as a black fog grew larger and darker in her mind until she slumped over.

The next day, the sound of Sal's car driving up penetrated the cobwebs of Robin's mind. She heard the crunching of the stones beneath his feet as he walked towards the house. The door swung open. Sal stood there, wearing that dazzling smile that melted her heart, arms outstretched with a wrapped present in one hand. "Hi, beautiful, miss me?"

She ran sobbing into his arms. He hugged her, rocking her and softly cooing. He leaned his head back, put a finger under her chin, lifting her face upward. He studied her red-rimmed eyes. "Honey, I've begged you to take antibiotics. I swear they'll help, even if the flu is a virus."

"No, no, it's not that. Beth. . .she's dead. Murdered in OUR house yesterday. And Frankie and Annie are gone, dead too, I guess. Oh, God, I'm so glad you're home."

"Beth dead? Murdered?" He said it in a shocked voice.

Robin sobbed out the story of the events of the last two days, while Sal stroked her hair and dabbed her eyes with his handkerchief. With a limp hand, she gestured toward the large bloodstain on the carpet.

Sal got up and studied the stain, his face ashen. "What are the odds?" he said.

"What?" she said, puzzled.

"Oh, nothing. It's just seems so impossible that someone, your best friend, could have been murdered in our own home."

"And Frankie and Annie. . ."

He waited for her to finish, but she just stared down at the floor, her face twisted in misery. "You should have called me; you shouldn't have had to deal with all this, alone."

"I tried calling you in Chicago, but you'd already left," she sniffled. "The police want to talk to you, too, although I told them you know nothing that could help."

He stiffened. "I'm sorry, baby. I had to fly to San Francisco. Damn, I should have told you, thoughtless of me. I wish I'd have been here for you. Well, maybe I can do something about Frankie and Annie. I'll call that investigator we use at the firm sometimes. He's amazing, can find anyone or anything." He looked up the number in his Palm computer and dialed. "Hi, this is Sal Kaufman. My wife is severely traumatized. She has a pair of pet geese that she adores – more than you can imagine – that have disappeared. I'd like you to find them. Spare no expense. TV, radio, newspaper ads, hire people to search. Whatever it takes." He paced back and forth as he listened. "Okay, I'll see you tomorrow morning. Bye."

Robin looked up at him; gratitude filled her eyes. "Oh, honey, thank you. Maybe we should hire him to help the police find Beth's murderer?"

He kissed her again, gently, on the cheek. He looked down at her with concern. "We'll see. You feel up to opening your present, or you want to wait?"

She almost managed a smile. "Thank you, baby. Maybe later. Why don't I make us a drink while you unpack?

He unpacked, put his shaving kit in the bathroom, then returned with the package. She opened it, a red flush appeared on her cheeks and neck as she realized it was a pair of crotchless panties and a garter set.

"Victoria's Secret. Like them? I'm sure you don't feel like doing anything, what with Beth and all...."

"No, really, it's fine. Just let me brush my teeth first." She took the tiny scraps of red silk with her to the bathroom.

She opened a drawer and grabbed her toothbrush and toothpaste, tried to squeeze something out of the flattened, empty tube without success. Looking for toothpaste, she opened Sal's shaving kit, surprised to see a prescription vial.

Penicillin? Dated two weeks ago, only a few pills left. On impulse she opened the door and approached him with the medicine vial. "Why do you need penicillin? What's wrong? Why didn't you just ask me for some? You know I have all those sample pills from work?"

His mouth flew open, a red flush crossing his face. His eyes narrowed and his lips tightened, but then at once his face changed to a picture of guilt and contrition. "Darling, sit down. I have something to tell you. Last month, one time and one time only, I was weak. This woman...she reminded me of you. Not as pretty and certainly not as smart, but something about her made me think of you. I'd had too much to drink...." He looked down at his feet, then looked at Robin with a helpless gesture.

Robin stared at him in disbelief. "You were unfaithful?"

He put his hand on her shoulder; she shrugged it off. "It won't happen again. It meant nothing, honest. And. . .well, apparently I got gonorrhea. I think that's what you have, not the flu."

"And that's why you have been harping on me to take antibiotics? So I can get rid of gonorrhea without knowing I ever had it, without knowing that my husband screwed some diseased whore and infected me?"

"I'm so sorry, baby. What are the odds? One screw-up and I gave the woman I love something so horrible. I'll make it up to you, hon, I promise."

Robin gasped for breath. Gonorrhea. . .she, a doctor that counseled the dirtballs who had sexually transmitted diseases. . .she might have, probably had, gonorrhea? Her throat constricted, as if his broken vows were strangling her. Her mouth felt dry and foul, tasting metallic. She ran to the bedroom, locking the door behind her as she crumpled to the floor in a fetal position, her bruised soul wailing.

Robin drove to Salinas the next day. She had made an appointment with a doctor in that town to get a culture and antibiotics. She could have gotten them free at her own doctor's office, but how could she explain? The shame, the embarrassment. Only tramps got gonorrhea, right?

She entered the doctor's office, startled to see a waiting room full of patients. She walked up to the receptionist's window. "Robin Kaufman here to see Dr. Mazzeo."

The receptionist handed her a form to fill out. "What was your problem again...doctor?"

Robin looked around, then leaned in and whispered, "Test for gonorrhea."

"Gonorrhea test," the receptionist bellowed, seemingly pleased to see the reactions on the faces of her fellow workers and waiting patients. Robin scurried to a seat, burying her red face behind a magazine.

As she walked into the house, she barely glanced at him, saying in a monotone, "Well, I finally got the damn antibiotics."

He nodded, his eyes pleading for forgiveness. "I bought you this. I know it doesn't change anything, but, well, I wanted you to have it." He handed her a French ceramic goose, beautiful and pricey. It looked just like Frankie. She clutched the statue to her chest and fled to the bedroom, closing the door behind her.

She sat on the bed, one finger tracing the outline of the goose, then noticed that her backpack was on the floor; it must have fallen off the nightstand. She reached inside to be sure that her tape recorder hadn't been broken. Found it and saw that the light was on. It was recording; the fall must have activated it. She rewound it, stopped and played it to see if the tape was now at the end of the police lecture. She was surprised to hear Sal's voice. He must have knocked it off when he was making a phone call.

Curious, she increased the volume. Sal's voice: "Remember that search for those two goddamn geese, well cancel it. Well, to tell you the truth, my wife was a bit hysterical, so I just wanted her to think you were doing this extensive search. You understand. I'd of course appreciate it if you didn't let her know I've canceled, you know, in case she calls or something. Thanks a lot, I owe you one." She stared at the tape, as if it would somehow give her an explanation. She gulped, a vague feeling of unease trying to rise to her consciousness, her skin prickly. She sensed that she shouldn't confront Sal with this, just wait and see how good a liar and actor he was. She put the tape recorder away, took a deep breath, then walked back to the living room.

Sal was hanging up the phone. Beth said, "Did you hear anything from the police yet?"

"No, I just made us reservations at Rocky Point. I know how you love their cheese bread. What do you say?" He grabbed his coat and opened the door, stepping aside with a deep bow and flourish with his hands directing her to exit. She said nothing, but floated ghost-like out toward the car.

As they drove, Robin stared out the window, and Sal prattled. What was he saying?

"...told me his deal to develop that land fell through, something to do with endangered salamanders, or was it red-legged frogs? Some damn thing. God said man should manage animals for Christ sake. What's more important, man or some damn salamander?"

She took a deep breath. "I just read about the clay plug that bears get in their intestines just before hibernation. It somehow stops the build-up of urine and toxins. By studying them, we can learn how to prevent kidney disease and diabetes. It's as if God gave us all the answers and cures; we can learn something from every animal, every plant." A mound of gray fur on the side of the road caught her eye.

"Oh, look a 'possum was hit. Stop! I need to check to see if there are any live babies in the pouch. Over half do, you know." She scooted over, grabbing the door handle, ready to jump out when he stopped.

Sal swerved toward the opossum and ran over it. Thump. Thump.

"Sorry, hon, I couldn't stop in time, dead anyway," he said.

"Bastard," she mouthed. Unrestrained tears fell down her cheeks.

Several minutes later they drove down the driveway to the Rocky Point Restaurant.

She got out and said, "You go ahead. I'm going to take in the view for a few minutes."

Robin stood on the cliff, listening to the pounding surf, her heart aching. Who was this man, she thought. They had been married for a year, dated only six months. Had he changed, or was she a damn fool, incapable of judging character? Thirsty, she reached into the car and took a sip from a bottle of water. A flock of birds flew overhead. Her head jerked skyward, the bottle slipping from her hands spilling to the ground. Could Frankie and Annie be among them? Of course not, you silly fool, she said to herself.

She stood there, enjoying the breeze on her face as she watched the antics of the seagulls. The sound of the ocean made her fidget. Damn, she had to go to the bathroom. She walked in through the back entrance, but was stopped by a young man outside the women's restroom.

"I've just mopped in there. Please wait ten minutes," he said. She was starting to feel woozy, sick to her stomach. He noticed her pained expression and said, "You can use the men's restroom if you want. No one's in there."

Robin nodded gratefully and dashed into the men's restroom. She really didn't feel well at all. She sat on the toilet, barely having enough strength to tuck her legs up. They felt like lead weights, as if they were someone else's. Her mind emptied, time passed by. Talking jolted her. Sal! That was Sal's voice. She tried to clear her muddled mind and listen.

Footsteps walked toward the stall next to hers then stopped. She tried to get it together enough to pull her legs up farther, and prayed. The steps stopped in front of her stall. Robin held her breath. She could see locks of his sandy blond hair hanging below the door as he peered underneath. The footsteps continued toward the urinals.

Sal was talking to someone. "Talk about a royal screw up! I'd say killing Robin's friend about takes the cake. What the hell happened, anyway? The bet was that you could use some of my Rohypnol so Robin wouldn't remember what happened. You could act out your fantasies. No one hurt, no one the wiser. I even left Chicago early so I could get rid of the damn geese so that you didn't have to deal with them."

His voice changed as if addressing himself. "I don't know why I didn't think to do it earlier. Gave them to a granola-type, you know, hippie guy." His voice shifted to a shout. "Then I come home to find out Beth is dead?"

"Well, how was I to know the woman in your house wasn't Robin?" the man whined. "She was even wearing the raccoon sweatshirt you said she'd probably be wearing, for Christ's sake. Things got out of hand. She kind of woke up. I tried to shut her up. Didn't mean to, but next thing I know, blood all over, and she's dead!" He started blubbering, his next words indecipherable.

Sal stopped him, his voice consoling. "Look, I know how it is. With all the times I've used that stuff, I've only had it wear off a couple of times. But when it did, you pretty much had to kill 'em or they'd ID you, and your ass would be in jail. We both would have been in a world of hurt if Beth had lived to tell the police. Listen, I've put some of that stuff in Robin's water in the car. She'll drink it on our way home, be perfect timing. Follow us home. You'll have the time of your life! Help you forget about that nightmarish night."

"You got any more of that stuff, 'case it wears off?"

Robin heard Sal slap the pocket of his jacket. "Never leave home without it."

She heard the bathroom door open and close, footsteps receding. She sat there stunned, slowly lowered her legs to the floor. An image of the dropped water bottle filled her mind. She felt heavy and paralyzed, but knew she had to get out of there fast. She opened the door and peeked out. Nobody. Robin dashed through the door and fled out the exit.

She tottered into the outside darkness. Head bent over, she paced back and forth, filled with fear, bewilderment, anger and sadness, most-of-all, sadness. Grief over the loss. Loss of her dreams for the golden years they were never going to share together, loss of the children and grandchildren they would never have, sadness for the loss of trust. She would never trust her judgment again. She would never trust anyone, period. But, by God, she wouldn't go out with a whimper. She straightened, determination flooding through her, and marched into the restaurant to Sal's table.

"Where the hell you been?" he growled.

"Sorry, but there's an injured seagull. I just have to catch it. It's chilly. Can I borrow your jacket, just for a minute. I'll be right back."

He looked at his watch, irritated, took his jacket off and handed it to her. "Okay, but hurry up. We don't have time to save the whole fucking world, you know."

She took the jacket and dashed outside, grabbing the small vial from the front pocket. She had no idea how much to use, but that bastard was going to at least know the terror of being drugged and vulnerable before going to jail. Looking skyward, she said, "This is for you, Beth." She put as much powder as she could hold between her fingertips, then let the rest of the vial's contents scatter in the wind.

She walked back into the restaurant and handed Sal his jacket. Just as he grabbed, she dropped it.

"Oops," she said. Sal stooped to retrieve the coat, and she put the powder into his wine. She asked the waiter for an order of cheese bread, and eyed Sal with hostile curiosity. He smiled uncertainly, not sure what to make of her mood, deciding to appear very engrossed in the menu.

After a few minutes, he grimaced in pain. "I need to go outside and get some fresh air," he grumbled as he lurched out of his chair. She waited, then followed in silence.

He bent over, putting his head between his legs, then straightened to walk in the direction of the cliff.

"I don't think you should go near the edge in your condition," she cautioned. Her voice startled him. He spun around. "Bastard! I want you to rot in jail, not have a quick death."

He looked at her, then patted his front pocket. Sudden realization filled his face.

"You bitch!" He grabbed her by the throat and squeezed. She struggled, but even though drugged, Sal was too much for her, his strength insane. She felt consciousness slipping away, when all at once she heard the sound of wings beating the air nearby. She tried to focus, then could swear she saw Frankie. And there was Annie!

The two geese attacked Sal, beating him in the face with their powerful wings and sharp bills. "Erhonk! Erhonk!"

Sal flailed with his arms, then stepped backwards into the darkness, his screams masked by the sound of the waves crashing onto the rocks below.

"Frankie! Annie!" The two geese settled to the ground next to her. Robin buried her head in their feathers, tears streaming down her face.

She stared at the cliff's edge and whispered, "What are the odds?"

Hacienda Good Karma

BY WILL PETERS

Hacienda Good Karma

BY WILL PETERS

"Aleta killed Hiram," she said.

Amused by her campy refusal to speak in the first or second person, Julius Bell drew a tissue from the box on his glass-topped conference table and handed it to Aleta Willoughby. "Sounds like misdirected blame to me, my dear. The cause of death was heroin overdose. You're not responsible for Hiram's addiction."

Busty, petite, and exuding a bohemian vibe Julius labeled fairy-tale chic, Hiram's elfin widow wiped her eyes and looked down at the miniature chocolate poodle on her lap. "If Julius knew the whole story, he'd understand."

As he absorbed Aleta's lilac perfume, Julius wondered if she sensed the "ifs" that were dancing in his imagination. If he weren't the jowly, white-haired probate lawyer who needed a cane to get around, would Aleta find him as attractive as he found her?

Ever since Hiram's father, Garth Willoughby, engaged Julius to prepare the family trust, Julius had followed the lives of Garth's sons, Hiram and Phillip. Garth was a big man in the Salinas Valley agribusiness. He owned forty thousand acres of Monterey County land, a string of warehouses from King City to Castroville, and operated a successful produce brokerage. Garth's acquisitive obsessions had left him no time for his wife. She withdrew into alcoholic isolation and had died when the boys were still teenagers.

Garth believed the way to prepare his sons to run the business was to start them at the lowest level. Hiram, the eldest, endured Garth's corrective criticism until he escaped into heroin addiction at nineteen. Several years and three residential cures later, Hiram returned to Willoughby Farms in middle management. His younger brother, Phil, never worked for the old man. He dissolved into the hippy life of Big Sur and lived in a stone cabin on a thousand acres Garth owned off the Old Coast Road, about fifteen miles south of Carmel. Phil called the place "Hacienda Good Karma."

Garth always said Aleta was the best thing that ever happened to Hiram. She had just the smarts Hiram needed to sit in the chief executive's chair. Garth admired Aleta's go-get-'em approach to running her Carmel art gallery and the generous way she used her powers of persuasion to launch the careers of many young artists. Garth often said, "Aleta's a damn fine lady."

When Garth died, Hiram took his place as the head of Willoughby Farms. Hiram made Aleta promise to keep her hands off. He wanted to "grow the business" his own way.

Aleta dried her eyes. "Hiram was ashamed that he couldn't fit into Garth's big shoes. Aleta tried to boost Hiram's ego, but Hiram knew she was pretending. After his judgment started to really hurt the business, Aleta was cruel to Hiram. She's the reason he used heroin again."

"Nonsense," said Julius.

She appeared not to hear him. "And Aleta hated how Hiram turned mean and tried to hurt Phil. It was like he wanted Phil to be miserable, too."

Julius nodded. "I know. He asked me to transfer the Hacienda to a land trust to stop Phil from living off the family."

"And when Hiram got loaded, Aleta hated him. She threw him out, Julius. She told him never to come back."

Julius knew his conference with Aleta Willoughby had reached its productive limit. "Why don't we schedule a time when you feel better to talk about the administration of the trust."

Aleta placed her small, jeweled hands to her forehead as if to check a mental list of subjects she wanted to discuss with

Julius. "That's another thing Aleta hates. Garth was cruel to give half to Phil and half to Aleta. The prize jumped right over Hiram and went to the prodigal son. Poor Hiram. Julius shouldn't have let Garth reward the bad brother."

"We don't tell our estate planning clients what to do. We do what they want."

She smiled. "That's why Aleta hates lawyers."

Julius was sure Aleta did not want to run Willoughby Farms. Her new gallery in New York, near the hub of the art scene, had only been open a couple of months.

Phil's wishes were harder to determine. Should the family business be sold and assets distributed? Did he want to come out of hiding to run Willoughby Farms? These questions triggered unsuccessful efforts to communicate with Phil. He had no telephone and Julius's several letters went unanswered for over two months. The longer the decision to sell Willoughby Farms was delayed, the more Julius was required to devote his attention to running the business. That responsibility crowded his law practice and disrupted his quiet solitary life. When August and September passed without a reply from Phil, Julius decided to pay a visit to Hacienda Good Karma.

At Bixby Bridge, a graceful arch two hundred feet above a wide rocky creek, Julius turned his Lexus east. After the first mile the dirt road dropped to a narrow, single-lane, creek crossing, and continued up the south face of the canyon through majestic stands of redwood. Julius told himself how grateful he would have been had his family left him such a big hunk of beauty. Those who want it, never get it; those who have it, commit suicide. Maybe Phil Willoughby was smart to get away from Garth.

Julius drove five more miles before he came to a heavy gate on a side road. His key opened the lock on the chain.

Beyond the gate big leaf maple and white alder trees shaded a road that ran parallel to a stream. Their density concealed the scrub and chaparral that covered the flanks of the ridge to the south. Within a quarter mile he drove through oak woods and an evergreen forest until he came to another gate for which he had no key.

Julius tried several predictable permutations on the four-number combination lock. He knew from his topographical map that Phil's cabin was about half a mile up the road. Leaning against the hood of his Lexus, he looked down at his Bally loafers, and contemplated the grinding pain that would fill his hip if he began walking.

The sound of rushing air and a splattering startled him. The shiny hood of his Lexus was drenched in red paint. Julius dropped behind the driver's side fender, wincing with arthritic pain. Judging from the splatter, the paintball was shot from the ridge above the stream.

"Next one's gonna be real. So just turn right around and drive out the way you came." The voice was deep and smokey.

"You don't understand. I'm the lawyer who wrote you the letters you never bothered to answer."

A second paintball careened onto the hood of Julius's car. "That's my answer. And don't even think about calling the cops, if you want to stay healthy."

Julius thought about calling the police for several days, until he decided to talk to Eddie Z instead. Eddie was a client who owned Cody's Bar in Carmel and used Julius for re-entry services. After a long history of undeclared income, Eddie needed to make peace with the taxman. Tax re-entry was one of Julius's specialties.

A suite of textured plaster rooms decorated with photographs of old Monterey, Cody's Bar was down a flight of stairs off Ocean Avenue. Its smoky fireplace and redwood tables evoked a homey, well-worn mood.

Eddie Z, a short, intense, leather-vested man in his early forties, wore an earring, wire glasses, and a two-day growth.

Over a club soda, Julius asked, "You know Phil Willoughby?"

Caution swept Eddie's face. "I've heard of him. Understand he's got a real screwed-up family."

"What do you mean?"

"You hear stuff. About Hiram's yen for smack and about his wife, the cutesy art critic. What's her name?"

"Aleta."

"That's the one. Why you interested?"

"Phil's about to get a big inheritance."

"He'll need it."

"Trouble?"

"A month ago I wouldn't tell you this, old buddy. But I like you. You saved my ass. How shall I say this? Phil's 'produce broker' just got popped. The word is Phil's real nervous."

"This broker have a name?"

"You didn't hear it from me. His name is Sal Tringali."

"And he deals in?"

"Everything." Eddie's eyes said the conversation was over. "The drink's on me."

When Julius returned from lunch, his secretary placed a phone message on his desk. It asked him to call a woman named Janet. The reference was Hiram Willoughby.

"I'm not comfortable talking about Hiram on the phone," Janet said. "My last class is over at three. I could be at your office at four-thirty."

"I'm pretty full up," Julius said, hoping he could deal with Janet on the phone.

"If we don't meet today, it will have to be in two weeks."

"Did you know Hiram?"

"Mr. Bell, I really don't want to talk on the phone. I'm violating an important tradition by calling you at all. Please respect my wishes."

"I'll make room for you at four-thirty."

Janet Stillman was in her late twenties, a plain-faced blonde with assertive eyes who taught English at Salinas High School. She was dressed in dark slacks and a long-sleeved white blouse. After a stiff greeting, she opened her purse. She placed a July 23rd news article about the discovery of Hiram's body at the Harvest Hotel on Julius's desk. "In AA, we're not supposed to talk about people who come to meetings, and especially not those who ask us to be their sponsors. I am violating Hiram's anonymity by talking to you."

"I can't promise to keep what you tell me in confidence."

"I accept that. I saved this article to remind myself that recovery is tough." Janet sighed. "Hiram wanted me to be his sponsor. He told me about you, his wife, and how she threw him out. More than anything else, he said he wanted to stop using so that she would take him back. When I saw this article, I figured he just couldn't do it."

"He had a long struggle."

"But something doesn't make sense to me, Mr. Bell. Two days ago, I started helping another man who was Hiram's dealer. I can't tell you his name. Let's call him Smith, okay?"

"Agreed."

"Smith tells me the day Hiram died he got a call from him, asking to meet. Smith had just sold Hiram an ounce of pure smack. That should have lasted a month. Anyway, they met at their usual place. Hiram didn't want more. He wanted to give the ounce back! Smith told him he had a no-return policy. Hiram didn't want his money back. He wanted something else."

"What?"

"He wanted Smith to promise to never sell to him again."

Julius was puzzled.

"So I asked myself, where did the drugs that killed Hiram come from? It doesn't make sense that Hiram would give up on his struggle with drugs the same day that he was so strong with Smith. It goes against everything I believe about recovery. It scared me. I can't give you an explanation for what happened to Hiram, Mr. Bell. I thought you might want to get one." Janet stood up and extended her hand. "Thank you for seeing me."

Detective Briscoe of the Salinas Police Department greeted Julius with the graying, well-fed complacency of a cop close to retirement. Briscoe had arranged the evidence gathered from Hiram's Harvest Hotel room on a table in a spacious evidence locker.

Julius did not know what he was looking for when he called the detective. He simply said he wanted to satisfy himself that the District Attorney's accidental death conclusion was correct.

Julius' curiosity took him first to a bindle of heroin inside an initialed plastic evidence bag. "You have a test report on this?"

"It's heroin with a dash of PCP," Briscoe said.

"And fingerprints?"

"The kit's clean, except for the prints of the deceased."

Julius examined the reusable syringe inside another plastic bag. The plunger, he inferred, could be operated by a silver ring. "Where did you find prints?"

"His thumb print was on the ring. His index and middle fingerprints were on the grip." The detective placed the autopsy fingerprints on the table next to the blowups of the prints taken from the syringe.

"Get any prints anywhere else in the room?"

"Not a one."

"Isn't that strange?"

"Not if he went there to shoot up."

Julius studied the fingerprint cards and the fingerprint

blowups for several minutes. "Do you have pictures of where he injected himself?"

Briscoe produced color photos of Hiram's right arm.

"Any idea which tracks are the freshest?"

Detective Briscoe's pencil pointed to two puncture wounds.

"Why would someone shoot up twice?"

"He wanted more." Briscoe smiled.

"How did the needle enter?"

"From his forearm toward his elbow," Briscoe pointed to the blowup.

"Interesting," Julius said.

"Typical overdose is the way we see it."

"Thank you very much."

When Julius got back to his office, he badgered Eddie Z until he agreed to give him Sal Tringali's phone number. After four attempts, Sal answered. "Mr. Tringali, you don't know me. We have an acquaintance in common."

Aleta's answering machine said, "It's six o'clock. Aleta's coming out of her lonely cocoon tonight. She's treating herself to a drive down the coast for a gorgeous sunset and an obscene steak at Rocky Point. She'll be back at ten. Bye."

If he hurried, Julius believed he could catch Aleta just as she was ordering.

Rocky Point Restaurant has the most spectacular views of any on the coast. When he was younger, Julius loved its generous drinks and cheese butter that changed a baked potato into a cholesterol time bomb. With difficulty, Julius navigated around moving bodies of the wait people in the narrow corridor between the guest tables perpendicular to the glass windows on the waves. Toward the back of the dining room he saw Aleta.

"Sorry to intrude."

"Julius's not intruding," she chirped. "Aleta always loves to see Julius. Can Aleta buy din din for Julius?"

"A drink'll do."

"The most important trustee is not hungry?"

"Actually not."

Aleta caught the waiter's attention. "Campari and soda for the pretty lady. The pretty lady doesn't know what The Trustee wants."

"Aberlour single malt, if you have it?"

"Of course," said the waiter.

"My grandfather used to make Aberlour before he came to this country," Julius said during the awkward silence before their drinks arrived.

Aleta raised her glass. "Here's to Julius's whisky-making grandfather and, of course, to Aleta. Tonight she is released from her sad cocoon and is a joyous butterfly once again." She spread her arms in a gesture of wings. "Now, Aleta insists that Julius entertain her with something fascinating."

Julius thought for a moment. "Okay. For one thing, I met Phil. He ran me off Hacienda Good Karma at gunpoint. A nasty sort of guy."

"Aleta's not surprised."

"No?"

"It's Phil's temperamental period."

"Does he have them often?"

"Once a year for several months. Pot growers don't like people around at harvest time. It's hard to know who to trust."

"I'm familiar with that problem."

"Did someone betray Julius?"

"Yeah. Once upon a time."

"Is it too personal to tell Aleta?"

"It's too personal to tell Aleta," Julius said, as he remembered his divorce. To change the subject, he asked, "Do you have any idea how Phil felt about Hiram?"

"Some. He knew Hiram wanted to throw him out of the Hacienda and he probably hated him for that."

"Enough to kill him?"

"Oooh." Aleta put her fingers to her lips in mock shock. "How did such a dark and scary question occur to Julius?"

"I talked to a teacher from Salinas. She was Hiram's AA sponsor."

Aleta looked surprised.

"She said that the day he died, Hiram gave his smack back to his dealer and made the dealer promise never to sell to him again."

"Does the teacher have a name?"

"Normally I'd tell you, Aleta. But the teacher broke an AA tradition to talk to me. I have to respect her wish to stay anonymous."

"So Julius thinks Phil killed Hiram?"

"Let me put it this way, I don't think Hiram killed himself."

"I don't like that thought."

"Yep, it's an ugly one."

Aleta held her Campari to her lips absent-mindedly.

"I think Hiram had visitors at the Harvest Hotel who brought drugs to the room. Whoever they were, they must have been very persuasive. They probably told Hiram they understood how hard it was to detox cold turkey. They might have even said withdrawing gradually would be easier. For a little camaraderie, the visitors wanted to do some, too, and fixed extra hits. But the visitors didn't shoot up. As Hiram was nodding, the visitors injected him again. When he was dead, the visitors put the syringe in Hiram's hand to make it look like he shot up twice, and then removed all traces of the visit." Julius sipped his scotch. "Have you ever been there, Aleta?"

"To the Harvest Hotel?"

"Yes."

"Never."

"And what's amazing is that all the physical evidence points to a voluntary overdose. I've got to hand it to Hiram's visitors.

They were really good." Julius smiled and picked up an olive from a dish on the table. "That is, except for the heroin found in Hiram's body."

"What about the heroin in Hiram's body?"

"It wasn't Hiram's usual stuff. He was a purist. The stuff inside him was junk. It had been laced with PCP. And you know what? Phil arranged that."

Aleta put down her glass. As if following a therapist's instruction, she took deep breaths. A smile spread across her face. She folded her petite hands. "When Aleta asks for fascinating, she gets it."

"You bet. And there's more. The drugs in Hiram's hotel room came from Sal Tringali, Phil's pot wholesaler. When Sal told Phil about an unusual heroin purchase, Phil told him to spike the smack with a little PCP just in case anyone needed to know where it came from."

"That sounds dumb."

Julius sipped more of his Aberlour and watched Aleta's forehead begin to glisten. "Maybe. Sal also told me that you, Aleta, were a regular cocaine customer of his. He said you gave it as party favors at gallery openings to give a little lift to the champagne."

Aleta's eyes iced with hatred.

"And the really fascinating development was my talk with the maid at the Harvest Hotel. She recognized your picture in the *Carmel Art Life* that I showed her. She saw you and your dog going into Hiram's room the day he died." Julius finished his Aberlour. "You've got to hand it to Phil."

"Why? Because he's a tricky motherfucker like you?"

"Exactly. Since you killed Hiram, you can't, by law, inherit under Garth's trust. The entire estate goes to the prodigal son." With the help of his cane Julius stood up. "Aleta should expect to hear from Detective Briscoe." He took a ten-dollar bill from his wallet. "For my drink," he said.

ORDER ADDITIONAL COPIES

Rocky Point Murders

QUANTITY	PRICE	SUBTOTAL
	$12.95	

MAIL ORDER FORM TO:

NOIR PRESS
P.O. 5277
CARMEL, CA 93921

NAME

ADDRESS

CITY   STATE   ZIP

PHONE

Please add 8.5% sales tax if you are a resident of the State of California.

ORDER TOTAL: _____

TAX: _____

* SHIPPING: _____

TOTAL: _____

Method of Payment ☐ Check   ☐ Visa   ☐ Mastercard   ☐ American Express

CREDIT CARD NO.   EXP. DATE

SIGNATURE

* $4.50 for one, add $1.00 for each additional book sent via UPS